W9-BDO-047

"What do you want to do with your life?"

Kyla had been afraid Chase was going to ask something like that. How could she say she was trying to beat the clock, to cram a lifetime of living into the few years she had left if...?

"Me? I'm always looking for the next adventure," she finally replied. "The one that'll make my knees knock and my heart pound. But I don't make big plans for the future. It's a good thing, or I'd be frustrated at being stuck in Kathmandu."

"You ought to see some things while you're here. I can recommend a good guide." He gave her a modest smile. "Me. Of course, I'm not in your league. Your tour group said you're the best guide in the Himalayas."

"You didn't believe that, did you? All trekkers feel that way about their leader after a trip. They think you're wonderful. They even fall in love with you a little bit and forget you made them walk that extra mile."

"I can't promise I won't do anything like that."

"Like forget you had to walk that extra mile?"

"Like fall in love with the guide."

Dear Reader:

Happy October! The temperature is crisp, the leaves on the trees are putting on their annual color show and the daylight hours are getting shorter. What better time to cuddle up with a good book? What better time for Silhouette Romance?

And in October, we've got an extraspecial lineup. Continuing our DIAMOND JUBILEE celebration is Stella Bagwell—with *Gentle as a Lamb*. The wolf is at shepherdess Colleen McNair's door until she meets up with Jonas Dobbs—but is he friend or the ultimate foe? Only by trusting her heart can she tell for sure. . . . Don't miss this wonderful tale of love.

The DIAMOND JUBILEE—Silhouette Romance's tenth anniversary celebration—is our way of saying thanks to you, our readers. To symbolize the timelessness of love, as well as the modern gift of the tenth anniversary, we're presenting readers with a DIAMOND JUBILEE Silhouette Romance each month, penned by one of your favorite Silhouette Romance authors. In the coming months, writers such as Lucy Gordon and Phyllis Halldorson are writing DIAMOND JUBILEE titles especially for you.

And that's not all! There are six books a month from Silhouette Romance—stories by wonderful writers who time and time again bring home the magic of love. During our anniversary year, each book is special and written with romance in mind. October brings you *Joey's Father* by Elizabeth August—a heartwarming story with a few surprises in store for the lovely heroine and rugged hero—as well as *Make-believe Marriage*—Carole Buck's debut story in the Silhouette Romance line. *Cimarron Rebel* by Pepper Adams, the third book in the exciting CIMARRON STORIES trilogy, is also coming your way this month! And in the future, work by such loved writers as Diana Palmer, Annette Broadrick and Brittany Young is sure to put a smile on your lips.

During our tenth anniversary, the spirit of celebration is with us year-round. And that's all due to you, our readers. With the support you've given to us, you can look forward to many more years of heartwarming, poignant love stories.

I hope you'll enjoy this book and all of the stories to come. Come home to romance—Silhouette Romance—for always!

Sincerely,

Tara Hughes Gavin
Senior Editor

CAROL GRACE

A Taste of Heaven

Published by Silhouette Books New York

America's Publisher of Contemporary Romance

For Carolyn,
who gave me the idea and so much more—
fun, friendship and all the food in her freezer
when she moved to Colorado.
This book's for you.

And for Craig,
who flamed the creative spark,
with love and thanks.

SILHOUETTE BOOKS
300 E. 42nd St., New York, N.Y. 10017

Copyright © 1990 by Carol Culver

All rights reserved. Except for use in any review, the reproduction or utilization of this work in whole or in part in any form by any electronic, mechanical or other means, now known or hereafter invented, including xerography, photocopying and recording, or in any information storage or retrieval system, is forbidden without the permission of Silhouette Books, 300 E. 42nd St., New York, N.Y. 10017

ISBN: 0-373-08751-9

First Silhouette Books printing October 1990

All the characters in this book are fictitious. Any resemblance to actual persons, living or dead, is purely coincidental.

®: Trademark used under license and registered in the United States Patent and Trademark Office and in other countries.

Printed in the U.S.A.

Books by Carol Grace

Silhouette Romance

Make Room for Nanny #690
A Taste of Heaven #751

CAROL GRACE

has always been interested in travel and living abroad. She spent her junior year in college in France, and toured the world working in the hospital ship *Hope*. She and her husband spent the first year and a half of their marriage in Iran where they both taught English. Then, with their toddler daughter, they lived in Algeria for two years.

Carol says that writing is another way of making her life exciting, and she often writes on the deck of her mountaintop home, which overlooks the Pacific Ocean and which she shares with her inventor husband, their daughter, who is now twelve years old, and their eight-year-old son. Carol is proud that writing runs in her family: her daughter has had stories published in her school magazine, and her son pens mysteries in his spare time.

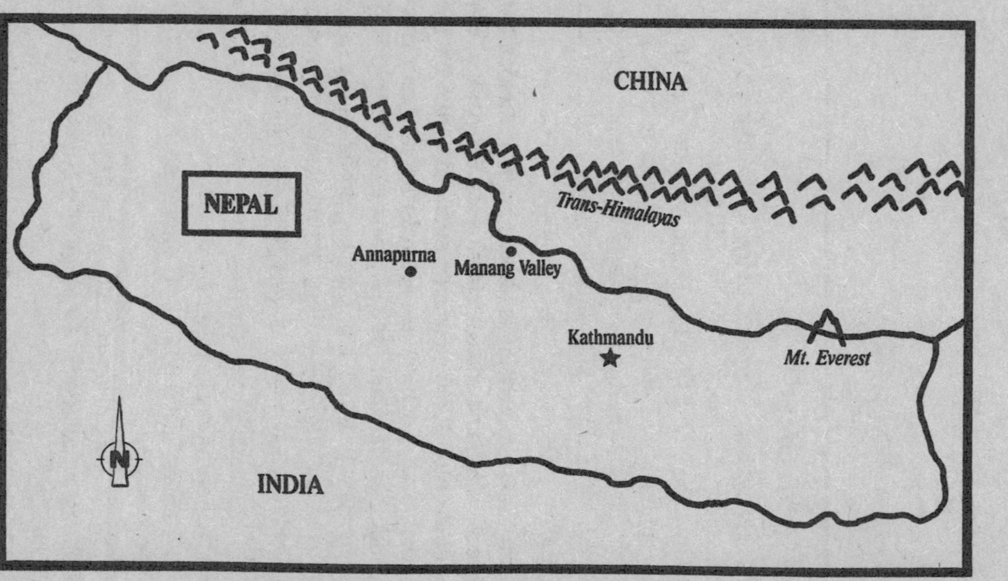
CHINA
Trans-Himalayas
NEPAL
Annapurna
Manang Valley
Kathmandu
Mt. Everest
INDIA
N

Prologue

The McDermotts of Friday Harbor always clasped hands and had a moment of silent prayer before Sunday dinner. Although Kyla Tanner hadn't been back to see her mother's family for a long time, she hadn't forgotten the tradition. Instead of closing her eyes, though, she looked around the polished oval table and studied the dear, familiar faces. Seeing the family again reminded her of the happy summers she'd spent on the island before her mother died.

"How much longer can you stay, Kyla?" Her cousin Beth's question broke into her reverie.

"This is my last day. I'm off after dinner."

"Where to, this time?"

"Nepal." She tried to sound matter-of-fact, but even she got chills of excitement thinking of scaling the giant Himalayas.

"Nepal?" Her aunt's voice rose with alarm. "Aren't you pushing your luck, young lady?"

"I think I'm incredibly lucky to get paid by Adventure Travel to do what I like to do. I feel like I ought to be paying them."

Aunt Mildred shook her head. "White-water rafting and hot-air ballooning. What would your mother have said?"

"She'd have said go for it. She would have done a lot more if she could. But she got married young, and then—" Kyla stopped abruptly. Even now, seven years after her death, it hurt to talk about her mother and her unfulfilled ambitions.

"I only meant," her aunt continued smoothly to cover Kyla's discomfort, "that the places you go are often lacking in proper medical care."

"Don't worry," Kyla assured her, taking a second helping of the excellent local salmon. "I carry a complete first-aid kit with everything from snake venom to antibiotics." She looked up and down the table, seeing a mixture of admiration and concern on the faces of her relatives. She must come more often to the old house on Puget Sound. If she had a home at all, this was it.

Out on a trail or in a kayak, she felt a sense of freedom. There nobody knew she lived under a cloud, which allowed her to pretend she didn't know it, either. She could imagine she was like everyone else, with the right to fall in love, get married and have children. Here in this house, they knew the truth about her and shared the same hopes and fears.

She reached across the table and covered her aunt's hand with her own. "I'm very careful," she said softly. "I know it sounds dangerous, but it isn't really."

Cousin Brian nodded his understanding. Looking at his husky body and cherubic face, no one would guess that he was just as likely to suffer from the fatal debilitations of the hereditary disease, Huntington's chorea, as the rest of them. "I know why you do what you do, Kyla. It's easier to take risks when you're already living with the biggest one of all."

"Maybe," Kyla replied quickly. She wasn't comfortable with Brian's analysis. She did what she did because she loved it. Maybe she had a sense of urgency that other people didn't; she was always haunted by the feeling that time was so precious you couldn't waste a single moment. She shifted uneasily.

"Nonsense," Uncle Jack interjected. "Even when she was a kid she took chances. Kyla was the one who swam out to the sandbar. She jumped off the rope swing and skinned her knees in the blackberry bushes. You don't expect her to change just because she grew up, do you?"

Brian shook his head vigorously and Kyla smiled at her favorite cousin. "You were not quite Little Lord Fauntleroy yourself," she told him. "I remember when you and I painted over the Keep Out sign on Agate Beach, then we climbed over the gate and filled our pockets with beautiful shiny stones. You came home covered with a mixture of paint and sand. Were you a mess! I told you not to do it, but you used to follow me everywhere."

Brian smiled. "I quit following you when you went to Easter Island. Now you have whole tours who follow you around the world. I always knew you'd do something exciting."

After dinner, they all assembled on the front porch where Kyla kissed them goodbye with tears in her eyes.

"How long can you keep running, Kyla?" her aunt asked as they drove to the ferry landing for the first leg of Kyla's journey to Kathmandu. "You'll have to stop and face it some day. Huntington's disease doesn't go away. Take the test. Find out if you have it. The others refuse, but you have more sense."

Kyla stubbornly shook her head. "If I stopped and faced it, I'd be no good at climbing or sailing or gliding. I admit I'm scared to take the test. I save my nerve for my job. I don't have enough to go around."

"Yes, you do," her aunt said quietly. "You have a lot of courage."

"No more than the rest of them," Kyla insisted.

At the landing, Kyla grabbed her suitcase from the back seat and gave her aunt a reassuring smile. "Next year, same time, same place?"

Mildred nodded and leaned over to hug her tightly. "I wouldn't say anything to you if your mother were alive, but I'm her sister. I've known you all your life...." Her words were muffled against Kyla's shoulder.

Kyla patted her on the back. "I know, and I understand. Don't worry about me. I had a wonderful time. Thanks for everything."

She waved to her aunt from the top deck of the ferry as it edged out into the sound. It wasn't until the car was a tiny speck on the shore that Kyla let the tears flow.

I *can* keep running, and as long as I can, I will keep running, she thought. "Why shouldn't I? I don't have to face the future until the future catches up with me."

Chapter One

Kathmandu was the last place Kyla Tanner had expected to be in the middle of October. Not that she didn't appreciate the exotic atmosphere of the fabled city, but she preferred the challenge of scaling the peaks that surrounded the fertile valley. Only two days ago she and the nine people in her tour group had been sitting around a campfire sipping *raksi* after a hard day of trekking. Now, here she was in a taxi in the middle of the bustling city, which seemed like another world.

Kyla blamed herself for Lillian's accident, for having chosen a difficult trail. On the other hand, she realized that anyone could slip on a loose rock and fall on her back. One of these days it could even be herself.

During her three years of leading tours everywhere from the South Pole to the Galapagos Islands, Kyla had been able to handle any emergency that came along with either moleskin or aspirin. But not this one.

She turned to look at the woman in the back seat and refrained from asking how she felt; one look at her ashen face and mouth twisted in pain was enough.

"We're almost there," Kyla said softly, "so just hold on a few more minutes. They say there's an American doctor there," she added hopefully.

Lillian's answer was a moan and Kyla breathed a sigh of relief when the taxi stopped in front of a low, sprawling building. The driver jumped out and opened the door.

"Dr. Chase's hospital," he announced proudly.

Kyla took in the cracked plaster, the peeling paint and the litter on the sidewalk. But whatever the place looked like, if there was an American doctor inside, they weren't going anywhere else; Lillian had reached the limits of her endurance.

She'd had an agonizing trip, carried by Sherpas over the mountains on an improvised stretcher, followed by a helicopter ride with Kyla in the jump seat beside her. This hospital with its crumbling exterior and the "famous" Dr. Chase were their only hope.

Kyla ran up the front steps and into the building. "Could I have a stretcher to move a patient in?" she blurted to the dark-skinned woman at the reception desk.

The woman looked up. "Does she have an appointment?"

Kyla took a deep breath and looked around the crowded waiting room. Every place was taken, old men in faded shirts with eye patches sat next to women in saris holding children on their laps.

"This is an emergency. We didn't have time to make an appointment. She had an accident in the mountains. We spent two days getting here. This woman is in terrible pain." Kyla leaned over the desk. "Could you please just tell the doctor we're here."

"Dr. Chase is in surgery," the receptionist said, smoothing a wrinkle in her white smock. "Is it an eye injury?"

Kyla considered the question. If it took an eye injury to get Lillian past this receptionist, well, she'd lie. She was getting that desperate. But before she had to stoop to deceit, a tall figure in a green surgeon's gown and mask appeared at the end of the tiled hallway. It had to be Dr. Chase.

At last here was somebody who would understand the gravity of the situation and do something about it. She breathed a sigh of relief. If he was surprised to find an American woman in wool stretch pants and a black turtleneck T-shirt with her brown curly hair in an uncombed tangle approach him, he didn't show it. What showed in his dark eyes was disapproval, and that shocked Kyla.

Anybody who looked the way she did and made her living the way she did was bound to attract attention around here. She wasn't the only woman guide in the Himalayas, but the others were older, more seasoned. They didn't have her high cheekbones and wide gray eyes and the deep throaty voice that made people stop and listen.

"Dr. Chase?"

Unfortunately, he seemed not the least bit interested in listening to anything she had to say. He didn't actually shove her out of the way, but he kept walking, taking giant strides down the hall, away from the lobby. Having hiked one hundred and twenty miles in the last three weeks, Kyla had no trouble keeping up with him.

"I've brought you a patient," she persisted, undaunted by his silence. "She fell and hurt her back on the other side of Lahkla two days ago."

He finally stopped and looked at her, his brown eyes heavy with fatigue, the lines in his forehead deepening into furrows. "Is this a tourist?" he asked with barely concealed disgust.

"Well, yes, but—"

"This is a Nepalese eye hospital. We treat the people who live here—people who can't afford to go anywhere else."

"But you're an American," she sputtered, "and this is an emergency."

"And if I'd wanted to treat rich, spoiled Americans, I would have stayed at home in America." His eyes swept over her body from the toes of her worn hiking boots to the top of her curls. When his gaze met hers again, she realized he wasn't so much hostile as tired. She wondered what the rest of his face looked like.

As if he'd read her mind, he pulled off his green cap and mask with an impatient gesture and dropped them into a nearby bin. Shaggy brown hair fell across his forehead. His mouth was full and sensuous, but he clamped his lips together. A deep cleft creased his chin. She gasped, feeling as if she'd stumbled onto a movie set. The man had that kind of looks.

Kyla swallowed hard. "I don't know if she's rich or not, but she's certainly not spoiled. We've been hiking fifteen miles a day and sleeping on the ground. The point is that she needs help and she needs it now. Couldn't you just have a look at her?"

He shook his head. "It wouldn't do any good. I don't have a single bed left in the hospital. Have you seen the waiting room? Those people have come from all over the country, and they're either blind or losing their sight. You think I'm going to drop everything for some woman who shouldn't be here in the first place?" He ran his hand through his hair. "Where is she?"

Kyla stood perfectly still, afraid to get her hopes up, afraid to show any emotion for fear he'd send her away. "In the taxi out in front. If you could just—"

"Have a look at her. I know. I heard you. I'll look at her, but that's all. I told you, there's no room for her here." He strode down the hall and through the lobby with Kyla at his side. The receptionist rose when she saw them coming.

"Doctor," she said with a look of worship in her brown eyes, "the family of Mrs. Khumjung are here to take her home."

"I'll be back in a moment," he replied over his shoulder.

No wonder the man is a tyrant, Kyla thought, going out the door one step behind him. He's treated like a minor deity around here, and he believes it. She was no stranger to arrogant young American doctors, or to gray-haired fatherly ones, for that matter. While nursing her mother through a long, degenerative illness and visiting her other stricken relatives in the hospital, she'd seen all kinds. Still, it was unpleasant to find this particular variety halfway around the world.

Chase looked at the woman in the taxi. She was obviously in great pain—so much so that he hesitated to turn his back on her. He should send her and the young woman who stood next to him on their way, but where to? The government hospital was across town, and... He wished the younger one wouldn't stare at him like that, with a mixture of hope, fear and determination in her eyes, and a look on her face that told him she wasn't used to asking for favors.

"All right," he snapped, angry with her for influencing him, angry with himself for giving in. "We'll bring her in and see what's wrong with her, but she can't stay."

They wheeled her in on a gurney, and after taking X rays, Chase sent the injured lady on to the ward and held the films up to look at them. The door of his office opened and the woman with the disturbing gray eyes walked in. He frowned. Hadn't anyone ever taught her to knock before entering? Not only did she walk in as if she owned the place, but she leaned over his shoulder and studied the pictures on the lighted stand.

"What do you think?" she asked, as if she were his colleague.

"Looks like a herniated disk," he said curtly, pointing to a spot near the lower curvature of the spine. "The disk between the fourth and fifth lumbar vertebrae is protruding."

Kyla inhaled sharply. "No wonder she's in pain."

Chase nodded and pointed to the X rays again. "These are the nerve roots leaving the spinal cord."

"Well, what can be done?" she asked, worry lines forming between her eyes. "She can't be moved." It was a statement, not a question, and Chase bristled; she seemed to think she knew more than he did. He switched off the light that illuminated the X ray, and turned to face her.

"She can't be moved, but she can't stay, either. I need that bed. I've given her something for her pain."

"What is it?"

Chase clenched his teeth. The sooner he got her and her friend out of this hospital, the better.

"Codeine." He paused. "Is that all right?" Then he watched with horror as her lower lip trembled. Good God, she wasn't going to cry, was she?

"Of course," she answered, pressing her palms together. "I'm sorry to be so edgy, but I can't help worrying. I'm responsible for her."

"Are you her daughter?" he asked, leaning against his desk, wishing he could take back the words as soon as he'd said them. The more he knew about her, the harder it was going to be to get rid of her. He watched with helpless fascination as her eyes changed from pale gray to the dark gray of the sky over the mountains.

"I'm the tour leader." She held out her hand. "Kyla Tanner, Adventure Travel."

He didn't want to shake her hand. He didn't want to touch her at all, but his eyes roamed over her tousled dark hair to her cheekbones to the round curves under her knit shirt. When he couldn't ignore her outstretched hand anymore, he took it. Her grip was as firm as he knew it would be, but her skin was softer than he'd imagined. There were no calluses on her palm. Of course not; the Sherpas did all the work on these tours, he reminded himself.

She was looking at him intently. "You asked if Lillian was rich. There's no point in lying. These tours are expensive and I imagine that her family would be very grateful to you for treating her and I suppose—" she looked around at the sparse furnishings, the cracks in the plaster walls "—that you could use a contribution for equipment or drugs... whatever."

He took a step backward. "Are you trying to bribe a member of the American Medical Society?" he asked incredulously.

The color rose from her neck up to her face and she straightened her shoulders. "Of course not," she replied icily. "I was just wondering if the hospital could use a donation. If you're too proud to accept money, perhaps there's someone else I could ask."

He couldn't believe the nerve of this woman. First she offered him money, now she was threatening to go over his head. "Not tonight there isn't," he informed her brusquely.

He'd been on his feet since six that morning, and he still had patients to see. He'd be damned if he'd put up with her another minute. "But maybe tomorrow you can find someone who will take your money. In the meantime your friend can stay here since Mrs. Khumjung is leaving. But in the morning you'll have to make other arrangements." He snapped off the lights in his office, and she followed him out to the front door.

He dismissed her with a curt nod and out of the corner of his eye watched as she disappeared into the smog and the evening traffic jam. Where was she going? To which of the new high-rise hotels in the Thamel quarter that catered to trekkers? How would she find a taxi in the chaos out there? He told himself not to waste his time worrying about her. She was obviously capable of taking groups of out-of-shape people up into those mountains and bringing them back down, if in worse condition. She could certainly get herself across town.

Kyla's taxi shot through crowded streets, past the Queen's Reservoir, narrowly missing pedestrians, beggars and young Tibetan people dressed in Western clothes. She barely noticed any of them. She was staring straight ahead, seething at the way she'd been treated by the arrogant Dr. Chase. The way he'd sneered at her offer to make a contribution to the hospital, as if it violated his lofty principles to accept money; and then had made her feel like a spoiled child—an unethical one at that. Her cheeks burned.

She'd like to see him at the foot of Mount Everest hiking half as well as poor Lillian at those altitudes. Actually, she wouldn't like to see him anywhere ever again. The man obviously thought he was God's gift to the medical profession, and he would probably be just as obnoxious if he didn't look like a soap-opera hero with his smoldering deep-set eyes and his five-o'clock shadow. He was unbearable. But how was Lillian going to get along without him?

At the hotel she found the members of her group waiting for her in the lobby to hear about Lillian. She refrained from telling them anything but the good news. "She's in a hospital with a herniated disk. There's an American doctor and he seems very capable." Never mind that he also seemed high-handed and unfeeling. "She's resting comfortably," she assured them, not mentioning that Lillian would rest comfortably only until morning when she'd be out on the street again.

The group had changed from boots and heavy sweaters into street clothes and wanted Kyla to go out to dinner with them—their first real meal since they'd been back. Kyla pleaded for half an hour to bathe and change.

After three weeks of washing in icy streams, Kyla was not going to let thoughts of Dr. Chase spoil her luxurious soak in gallons of hot water. She couldn't help but think of Lillian, though, and decided that when they returned from the restaurant, she would call the Adventure Travel office in California so they could inform Lillian's relatives. They needed to send someone over to bring her home. Then Kyla would be off to lead a group of white-water rafters on the Yangtze River. She was eager to be on her way. She didn't like being stuck in some city between trips. It gave her too many opportunities to wonder how much more time she had left to test her nerve and skill.

After she dried off with a huge fluffy towel she dressed in a clean pair of stretch pants and a hand-knit lavender sweater, then led her group to her favorite restaurant, the Yak and Yeti. The maitre d' remembered her and Kyla was glad to see her group responding to the dark, friendly atmosphere and admiring the climbers whose pictures covered the walls. From their table in a quiet corner, Kyla stared at a photograph of Sir Edmund Hillary with his Sherpa guide. Had Sir Edmund felt the same restlessness she did, the same need to be on the move someplace new and experience the thrill of discovery? Even if he had, he couldn't have possessed her sense of urgency.

"Kyla." The voice of her youngest hiker, Mary O'Dwyer, brought her gaze back to the table. "There's a man over there who's been staring at you ever since we came in. Haven't you noticed?"

Kyla shook her head. "Where?" She casually looked around the room, holding a glass of the local rice wine in her hand. There in the far corner was a man with his back to her. There was something familiar about the set of his shoulders and the way his shaggy hair touched the collar of his jacket.

But who could it be? None of her friends was in town right now. Then he turned to face her and their eyes met and held. She set her glass down so hard the pale liquid sloshed onto the tablecloth. The doctor... She held her napkin up to her mouth, but what she really wanted to do was to crawl under the table and hide.

"I think I know who you mean," she muttered to Mary. Of all the restaurants in Kathmandu, why did he have to pick this one?

"You've been keeping something from us." Bill Marvin twisted his head around for a look.

"Please," Kyla begged, her face turning crimson, "if you'll just turn around and act normal, I can explain."

He obeyed and all eight pairs of eyes looked expectantly at her.

"Well," she said, making an effort to sound normal, "that looks like Lillian's doctor over there. He probably recognized me, so that's why he's been staring." She picked up a chapati from the bread plate and buttered it nonchalantly.

"He's all by himself," Mary remarked. "Shouldn't we invite him to join us? The least we can do is buy him a drink to thank him for taking care of Lillian."

"Oh, no," Kyla protested. "He doesn't want to be thanked. He's not that kind of doctor." And you don't want to know what kind he is, she thought.

"I can't stand to see somebody eating alone," Bill protested and stood.

Kyla closed her eyes to block out the sight of the gregarious Bill approaching the unapproachable Dr. Chase. Of course he wouldn't come, but it was still embarrassing. He might think she'd sent Bill over. When she couldn't stand the suspense anymore, she looked up and saw Bill shaking hands with the doctor and, to her amazement, bringing him back to the table.

Chase had to admit she was something to look at. Even from across the room her face glowed in the light from the gas lanterns on the walls. But that was no reason to join them for dinner. He had no intention of saying yes to the amiable young man who'd invited him. He wasn't lonely. He didn't mind eating alone; he did it all the time, and he liked it.

Most of all, he didn't want to eat with a group of trekkers who thought nothing of cutting down precious trees for their campfires. Without thinking of anybody but themselves, they denuded the countryside and hired the farmers out of the fields to be their porters. So why in hell was he standing at their table being introduced and shaking hands with everybody in their group?

"What a surprise," he heard Kyla Tanner say in her throaty voice. "I didn't know you were here."

He held her hand for the second time that day and looked at her. Liar, he thought. You saw me and I saw you.

She blushed as if she'd read his thoughts. "I mean, I didn't recognize you with your clothes on." As soon as she'd said that, she wished she hadn't. His eyebrows shot up and he opened his mouth as if he were going to make a suggestive remark, but the laughter that bubbled forth around the table cut him off. The group made room for him between Bill and his wife. Kyla gritted her teeth.

She usually loved these celebrations at the end of a trip. She would look around the table at the faces, knowing that they'd faced high mountains and different food and customs and come through it. But tonight she couldn't look around without catching the eye of the imperious Dr. Chase. Even if she looked at the ceiling she couldn't escape the conversation.

"You should have seen Kyla pulling me across a log bridge with both hands," Bill's wife was saying. "She walked backward, I walked forward. She kept telling me I could do it, but I couldn't have done it without her. I'm such a coward. Kyla's fearless."

Kyla opened her mouth to protest, but Elizabeth, the schoolteacher, chimed in. "Remember when the cook got homesick and left and Kyla had to bake the chapatis on the hot rocks?"

"And turn the goat on the spit?" Bill added. "She's going to make some nomad a great wife."

Kyla squirmed uncomfortably. The more they talked about her, the more frequently Dr. Chase's eyes sought hers. The dubious look on his face seemed to be saying, *This can't be you they're talking about*. She was glad her group had happy memories of the trip, but the dinner was beginning to sound more like a testimonial than a farewell.

She looked longingly at the front door, but they weren't finished with her. yet.

"She's the best guide in the Himalayas," Marty said. "And the most generous. When I smashed my toe she gave me the last of her brandy."

"That's what the brandy's for," Kyla insisted. "Medicinal purposes." She looked down the table and found Dr. Chase staring at her with disapproval in his eyes.

"Speaking of medicine," she went on quickly, "I'll bet Dr. Chase has some interesting stories to tell." She smiled to herself as all eyes turned in his direction. She felt a twinge of guilt at his uncomfortable look, but she told herself he shouldn't have joined them if he didn't want to be sociable.

"Is your family here with you?" Mary asked pointedly, and Kyla winced. Mary was trying to find out if he was married, and now he'd think... Oh, what did it matter what he thought. If they got through the dinner without talking about her anymore, she'd be happy.

She could have told Mary that he wasn't married. No woman in her right mind would put up with his ego. You could tell by looking at him—which she was doing despite her efforts not to—that he was the kind of doctor who was married to his profession, to the idea of helping people, but who hadn't the compassion that should accompany it.

Chase shook his head. "My father's a doctor," he explained. "He'd be here himself if he didn't have a practice and my mother to support. I'm lucky—" he paused and looked down at his hands "—I have no dependents and no house payments, so I can afford to do what I want. And this is what I want to do."

Bill's wife's eyes widened. "You mean you don't get paid?"

He grinned, and Kyla blinked in astonishment.

"Oh, yes," he answered. "Patients pay what they can. Yesterday I got two live chickens and the day before, a pound of yak butter. So I won't starve."

Kyla smiled in spite of herself and the others laughed. Was this man who was smiling and charming the socks off the members of her group the same one who'd been so rude to her in the hospital? Maybe he had a split personality like Dr. Jekyll and Mr. Hyde. He even looked different to-night.

He'd shaved, and without the dark shadow on his face he looked less brooding and more relaxed. Maybe it was her fault he'd looked tense and angry. He caught her staring at him and she glanced away quickly.

"Where's home?" Mary asked him.

"California."

Mary looked delightedly from the doctor to Kyla and back again. "Kyla's from California. Where in Califor-nia?"

"Piedmont."

Mary nudged her. "Isn't that near where your father lives?"

Kyla firmly shook her head. "Nowhere near Piedmont. We're miles apart," she said with so much feeling that Mary drew her eyebrows together in puzzlement.

When Kyla yawned and looked at her watch, Bill sug-gested they stop at the Rum Doodle for a drink, and in-vited Dr. Chase along.

"Call me Chase," he told Bill, but his eyes sought Ky-la's. "The Nepalis can't pronounce my last name, Cun-ningham, so they call me Dr. Chase, but it's really my first name."

The others could call him Chase—they could call him whatever they wanted—but Kyla didn't intend to call him anything at all. She said goodnight to her group in front of the restaurant while they waited for separate taxis. They knew she had to call home and explain about Lillian, but they tried to persuade her to have a drink with them anyway.

Kyla resisted. Tomorrow they would leave Kathmandu on the afternoon plane, and if she didn't get Lillian settled she wouldn't be on it. Which meant she wouldn't be in California in time to meet the members of the rafting trip on the Yangtze.

She didn't know if Chase was going with them to the Rum Doodle and she told herself she didn't care. She left him standing on the sidewalk frowning at her, his hands stuffed in his pockets. She watched him until a group of teenagers wearing stereo headphones crossed the road and blocked her view.

When she reached her hotel room, she kicked off her shoes and placed the call while sitting cross-legged on the bed. The office staff of Adventure Travel found Lillian's file and an emergency number of a brother in Bangor, Maine. They would phone him and call Kyla back. Adventure Travel liked the idea of Lillian being under the care of an American doctor. Kyla refrained from telling them he didn't want her under his care. She would worry about that in the morning.

But within the hour Kyla learned that Lillian's brother was a seventy-year-old man with emphysema. Would Kyla stay until they got somebody else? They would find someone else to do the China trip for her. Her heart sank, and her hand gripped the receiver so tightly her fingers were numb when she hung up. She had to stay here in this valley polluted with fumes and overcrowded with pilgrims and tourists while the mountains and rivers of the world were calling to her!

For anyone else, a few days' wait was a mere inconvenience. But Kyla looked on every day as a gift. She'd taken nothing for granted since her mother had died. She wanted to live every day to the fullest. And hanging around Kathmandu was not living; it was stagnating.

Chapter Two

It was only nine o'clock in the morning but already the sun threw shadows across the asphalted street where Kyla was standing in front of the run-down hospital. She stepped around a fruit vendor's stand and looked up at the double doors to the waiting room. After a restless night she was not looking forward to another confrontation with Chase. At midnight she'd had another conversation with Adventure Travel, then a late-night farewell drink with the group in Mary's room.

She found out that as incredible as it seemed, Chase had gone with them to the Rum Doodle.

"I think he's lonely," Mary remarked, handing Kyla a glass of Chinese beer.

Kyla shook her head. That was not how she would describe him. It would be something like "contemptuous"—of all the rich, spoiled Americans. She was surprised they hadn't noticed it. But that didn't explain why he went with them.

"He asked about you," Mary confided, a sparkle in her eyes.

"Uh-huh, I'll bet. He hadn't heard enough about me at dinner. What did he ask? When I was leaving?"

"When, why and where," Mary confirmed happily.

"I hope you told him I have a job to do. That I'm leaving as soon as I possibly can, if that's any comfort to him." Kyla swirled the beer around in her glass.

Mary grinned. "We told him about how you've got mountains to climb and rivers to cross."

Kyla smiled. Maybe she should have kept her thoughts to herself, instead of joining in the late-night discussions around the campfire.

Mary emptied her bottle. "Why didn't you tell us he looked like that?" she asked.

"I didn't notice what he looked like," she assured Mary, wishing she *hadn't* noticed the little lines at the corners of his eyes or the set of his jaw. Knowing these details somehow made their battle over Lillian more personal—and it made her feel she was losing control.

Mary frowned in dismay. "If you tell me you didn't see that he had eyes that could melt the snows on Annapurna, I'm going to give up on you." She put her hands on her hips. "Come on, Kyla, what are you waiting for? Who are you waiting for? Is there somebody back home?"

Kyla shook her head. "There's nobody there or anywhere. My whole life is my work, and that's the way I like it. I take them both one step at a time, one day at a time." Kyla broke off, embarrassed to be sounding philosophical. A few minutes later she said good-night to the group and went back to her room.

Now, standing in the dusty street in front of the hospital, she looked off in the distance at the white mountains rising above green ones, and fought off a wave of self-pity.

How could she feel sorry for herself when Lillian was lying helpless in that hospital? The mountains would still be there tomorrow and next week, too. And she would be there to climb them. If she had to miss today's flight, she could meet her new group in Beijing next week. She would check the flight schedules as soon as she left the hospital.

The waiting room was again full to bursting. The same woman in charge gave Kyla a cool, appraising look as if she'd stolen more than just one of their hospital beds. Or maybe she didn't recognize Kyla with a clean face and her hair combed. The receptionist finally pointed toward the women's ward.

Kyla stepped around a woman with a white bandana tied over her hair scrubbing the yellowed tiles on the floor. The sharp smell of antiseptic assaulted her nostrils and filled her with memories of other hospitals and other diseases too painful to think about.

She wanted to turn and run out the front door for some fresh air, but when she pulled the small curtain back from around Lillian's bed and saw her weak smile, Kyla felt a stab of guilt. How could she even have thought of deserting her?

Kyla set her straw bag on the end of the bed and took out a bunch of small sweet bananas, a bag of almonds and some magazines from the hotel newsstand.

"When can I leave?" Lillian asked eagerly. Kyla didn't have the heart to tell her the real problem was how long could she stay.

"That's what I'm going to find out, just as soon as I find your doctor."

"He was here early this morning with another doctor. But he asked me so many questions about my back I forgot what I wanted to ask him."

So, even though he disapproved of Lillian being there he wasn't ignoring her. And even though he'd been out late with her group last night, he'd already been here working for hours while she was having another bath and a leisurely breakfast. Even when he wasn't around, the noble Dr. Chase had a way of making her feel ashamed.

"What did you think of him?" Kyla sat carefully on the edge of the bed.

"He's wonderful." Lillian leaned back against her pillow. "He examined my back and explained all about my vertebrae." She reached for a piece of paper on the stand next to her bed. "He even drew me a picture of my disk. We're lucky we came here, Kyla. We're lucky he was here."

Kyla nodded and eased Lillian into a more comfortable position. Luck, she mused, as she walked down the hall toward the operating room in search of Lillian's "wonderful" doctor. The Hindu god, Vishnu, would never agree to that. He'd say it was fate.

At the staff meeting that morning Chase was surprised that none of the Nepalese doctors objected to admitting an American patient—especially when he mentioned insurance money and a possible gift to the hospital. He couldn't blame them for ignoring official policy and the fact that they were shorthanded and needed every precious bed; the hospital depended on charity for survival. But he wished he hadn't been so self-righteous yesterday with Kyla.

She had annoyed him with the way she had walked in and tried to buy special treatment. He thought he'd left that kind of woman behind when he came to Nepal. He'd been feeling so good about leaving that world, so good about the work he was doing here, so in tune with the people of this valley. And then she'd entered his hospital and shattered his sense of well-being and his routine.

Take last night, for example. As a rule he never sought out Americans, never went to places like the Yak and Yeti for dinner or the Rum Doodle for a drink. So why, he asked himself, had he done it last night? And why did he glance up after each operation this morning and look through the small window in the swing door of the operating room as if her face would suddenly appear there? And when it did, why did he look away so quickly that he wasn't sure it was really her?

Three nurses left this morning to go home for the Festival of Dasain, so every cataract operation took twice as long. When he'd finally finished the fourth one, he went out into the hall and found Kyla Tanner leaning against the wall waiting for him. She looked more like a gypsy than a mountaineer today. The creamy cotton of her loosely woven peasant blouse clung to the curves of her breasts and made it impossible for him to look anywhere else.

When he'd first seen her yesterday in layers of heavy clothing covered with red clay dust, he didn't know she could look fragile or vulnerable; but now, as she straightened and walked up to him, he had an irrational urge to put his arms around her and tell her that everything would be all right.

He kept his hands at his sides. "She can stay." He answered her question brusquely before she could ask it. "But only if you're willing to do what our patients' families do."

"Of course," she said, her gray eyes meeting his.

"Families provide the food, since we have no kitchens here. And they take care of the patients, especially now at festival time. By tomorrow all the nurses will be gone to spend the holiday at home."

"As long as I'm here, I'll do whatever is necessary," she assured him so readily, he knew she had no idea what she was in for.

"And how long will that be?" he asked.

"Just until the travel company finds someone to replace me." She looked at her watch. "I'm scheduled to lead a rafting trip to China next week."

He looked at his watch. "And I'm scheduled to remove another cataract in five minutes." And another after that, he thought. And I'm already behind schedule and without any help. He looked at her again. She held her hands in front of her, her long slender fingers laced together. Their eyes met. "You said you'd do whatever was necessary. . . ." He hesitated.

"Yes, of course."

"I could use some help in the operating room."

She gasped and he reached for her hands, holding them firmly. "Your group thinks you're fearless. They said you can do anything."

"No, I'm not. I can't. Besides, I wouldn't know how to do it. You have to have special training."

"You don't need training. You need a steady hand." He was acutely aware that he still held her hands. They were warm, steady and capable.

"That's just the trouble. I don't have one. I mean not in there I wouldn't. And I can't stand the sight of blood. I might faint or throw up." She bit her lip.

"Oh, come on, don't tell me you've never seen blood before out there on the trail. You don't look like the squeamish type to me."

She raised her chin and looked him in the eye. "Of course I've seen blood. It's hospitals that bother me. I hate them. I'm sorry. I'd like to help you, but I can't."

Lots of people hate hospitals, he thought. They hated the smells and the sight of sick people so much they refused to go near one, even to visit friends or relatives. Was Kyla

Tanner that type? Whatever type she was, he needed her. He tightened his grip and pulled her toward him roughly.

"There are people out there who can't see and who are waiting for me to give them back their sight," he said. "Are you going to turn your back on them? I'm only asking you to hand me the instruments. You don't even have to look at the patients."

Her eyes turned so dark they looked black and her face paled under the fluorescent light. She stood staring at him for a long moment, then she moistened her lips with her tongue.

"All right," she whispered, and he released her.

"You'll be fine," he assured her in a normal voice. "I'll show you where to scrub and change and I'll tell you what I want you to do."

A few minutes later, when he saw her wide, frightened eyes above the green mask, he almost changed his mind. What right did he have to take some woman off the street into surgery with him? Did he really trust her not to faint? Would she follow orders? From what he could tell, she was more used to giving them than taking them. Did he need someone that badly? Or was he just trying to test her, to show her that his work took as much courage as hers?

Kyla's fingers were cold inside the rubber gloves. She would rather have scaled the north face of Mount Everest than look at a surgeon's knife. It was only the commanding expression in Chase's dark eyes that kept her there in the operating room, that made her advance toward the table where the patient lay covered with green cloth, instead of backing out the door.

The instruments were laid out next to her and at his direction she handed them to him as mechanically as a robot. She told herself not to watch, but she couldn't tear her eyes away as Chase lifted the delicate cornea with the forceps she gave him.

He pointed to a smaller instrument. She gave it to him, then leaned over to observe him remove the cataract-clouded lens from under the cornea and replace it with a new, clear, artificial lens. Her knees shook as he lowered the cornea, but she forced herself to keep her hand steady when she picked up the needle he needed. Her heart pounded as he stitched the cornea to the patient's eyeball with a ring of tiny sutures.

After the procedure, she followed Chase out of the operating room, feeling as if she'd seen a miracle. Her hands, which had remained steady for the fifteen minutes she'd been working with Chase, started shaking so hard she could barely get the tight gloves off.

Chase glanced at her from the other side of the sink where he was peeling off his own gloves.

"Not so awful, was it?"

"No, no," she answered breathlessly. "You're very good."

"You weren't so bad yourself." He took off his mask and cap and she looked at him as if she'd never seen him before. She almost forgave him for being overbearing. No wonder doctors thought they were gods—they performed miracles.

Silently they washed their hands together at the sink. Then he took her arm. "Come outside with me in the yard. I want to show you an example of what you've just done."

She nodded wordlessly, conscious of the pressure of his hand, the warmth of his fingers on her skin.

Behind the hospital in the large yard, canvas tents had been set up and dozens of patients and their families were eating lunch at rough wooden tables under the trees. Chase led Kyla to one of the tables and introduced her to a man with a gauze bandage over one eye.

"Mr. Amatya was operated on last week. He was blind in his left eye. His family is here waiting to take him home. I promised to come out and take off his bandage as soon as I could."

The Amatya family gazed expectantly at Chase, who sat down next to his patient on the wooden bench and gently removed his dressing. There was a hushed silence and Mr. Amatya blinked. His face creased in a hesitant smile. He looked at his doctor and when Chase nodded encouragement he glanced around. His smile deepened and his relatives crowded around him, laughing and crying.

Kyla turned away to hide her tears.

"It makes it all worthwhile, doesn't it?" Chase asked.

She nodded. "The look on his face..."

"Will you do it again?" His expression dared her to say no.

"Now?"

He smiled and the lines at the corners of his eyes fanned out. He crossed his arms. "No, tomorrow. Since you'll be here anyway."

Tomorrow. She could do anything tomorrow. If she was still there, that is.

"Yes, if you need me."

"I'll need you." His smile had vanished, he was serious again.

A puff of smoke from a charcoal brazier blew toward them. Kyla sniffed the air. Families were cooking lunch and suddenly she was ravenous. "I'd better get Lillian something to eat."

"And yourself," he ordered.

She waited for him to suggest something, like where to go for food and how to get there, or maybe even go with her.

But he just stood there looking at her until she turned and walked through the hospital and out onto the street. Just down the road was a tea shop where she bought sandwiches and fruit, then hurried back to eat with Lillian.

They spent the afternoon discussing ways of getting Lillian home when the time came, although Chase had told Lillian it would probably take several weeks before she could be moved safely.

The waiting room was empty when Kyla left. There were no patients and no doctor in sight. She glanced down the hall toward the operating room and the receptionist answered her unspoken question.

"The doctor has already left."

"Yes, of course." Kyla walked nonchalantly out the front door and caught a taxi back to the hotel.

In her room, she called Adventure Travel, and they told her what she already knew deep down in her heart. There was nobody available to come to Kathmandu and take her place with Lillian at the hospital. Someone had been found to lead her China group, though, and she would remain on full salary while she stayed here. *If* she would stay. How could she say no?

She forced herself to go out to dinner, although she had no appetite. At sunset the Himalayan peaks glowed in the distance beyond the city, but the sense of wonder Kyla usually felt at the magnificent sight was missing. Instead she felt hemmed in, trapped, a prisoner in the valley.

She dropped a handful of coins into a beggar's hands as she left the small restaurant where she hadn't tasted a bite she'd eaten. Up in the mountains she never felt lonely, but here among the throngs of foreign trekkers and urban Nepalis she felt as out of place as the Tibetan refugees who crowded into the city every day.

Instead of going back to face the four walls of her hotel room she walked through the narrow streets, passing open stalls displaying carpets, herbs and wooden carvings. She bumped into a businessman with a briefcase and passed a woman leading a bull with a garland of flowers around its neck. The air was thick with smog, the smells of garlic and ginger mingling with rancid yak butter.

As she turned down a small lane to escape the exhaust fumes from a tour bus, she suddenly stumbled on a curb. Her heart leaped to her throat as an icy fear gripped her. Was this it? Was this stumble a first symptom of the beginning of the end? She forced her legs to keep moving. To test her balance she walked a crack in the pavement. She was concentrating so hard, she barged into a goldsmith's stall where bright rings and bracelets were stacked next to a blazing forge. She pressed her hands against the counter and stared into the flames for a long moment.

When her legs felt steady again and her heart rate was back to normal, Kyla murmured a few polite words in Nepali to the goldsmith and carefully made her way back through the crowded streets to the hotel, setting up tests for herself along the way.

Cobblestones, gutters and manholes were all obstacles to navigate. As her steps grew surer, her confidence slowly returned. When she finally saw the lights of the hotel before her, she felt a surge of relief so strong she forgot to be depressed about staying in Kathmandu. Instead of feeling hemmed in by the walls of her small room, she felt safe and secure. Exhausted from her walk, she fell into a deep sleep.

In her dreams a surgeon wearing a green mask and holding a scalpel in his hand leaned over a patient and told her he wouldn't treat foreigners. When Kyla realized that the patient was herself lying under a sheet on an operating table, she tried to scream and pull off the sheet. She had to tell him he was wrong; that she wasn't sick and didn't need a doctor. But the words caught in her throat, and she woke up in a cold sweat, tangled in the sheets of her hotel bed.

After a shower she dressed quickly and stopped at the coffee shop for two Western-style breakfasts to go, then took a taxi to the hospital. Kyla carefully arranged Lillian's breakfast on a metal tray and again felt ashamed of her own impatience. And once again she was forced to listen to a glowing tribute to the wonderful doctor who had stopped by to see Lillian as he was making his rounds that morning.

"He said you were a big help to him yesterday, and I told him I wasn't surprised. Tour guides have to be able to handle everything. I know, I've been on these before. But you're the best, Kyla, the best in the business. Everyone says so. That's why everyone wants to go with you."

Kyla looked down at her toast. "You didn't tell Dr. Chase all that, did you?"

"Of course. Why not? He was interested." Lillian shifted and winced with pain.

Kyla leaned forward, frowning in concern. Lillian gave her a weak, reassuring smile.

"Just so long as you didn't tell him I was fearless." Kyla smiled back.

Lillian shook her head. "No. I imagine everyone's afraid of something. Even you."

Kyla settled Lillian in the most comfortable position possible, then walked quickly down the corridor toward the operating room. Maybe everyone was afraid of something, but that something didn't follow them relentlessly from place to place, looking over their shoulder, breathing down their back. Every time she slurred a word or stumbled the way she had last night, the fear rose and threatened to overtake her.

She stopped abruptly. Chase was standing outside the swing door to the O.R., his arms crossed, glowering at her just as he had in her dream.

"You're late."

She grimaced. No matter how many kind words Lillian had said about her, it was obvious he still thought of her as someone whose function was to carry out his orders.

"I'm sorry," she said with forced politeness, "but when you asked me to come today, you didn't mention a time."

"I'm mentioning it now. We start at six-thirty." He held the door open and motioned for her to take her place at the sink. She stood helplessly with her arms out in front while he pulled the green gown around her and tied the strings. His hands brushed against her back and sent a jolt of current down her spine.

She watched him scrub out of the corner of her eye. His hands were wide. His fingers looked impossibly large to have done the delicate work she'd seen him do yesterday. Yet he had done it, and she'd seen the results. Was he really an ophthalmologist? If so, how did he know about slipped disks and spinal injuries? And what was he doing here? What was he running away from?

"How long have you been here?" she asked casually.

"Since six-thirty."

"Yes, I know. I'll be here tomorrow at six-thirty."

"It won't be easy if you're hanging out at night in bars with trekkers."

She angrily set down the bar of soap. "I don't hang out in bars...with anyone. You're the one who went to the Rum Doodle the other night, not me!"

His eyes narrowed but he continued his scrubbing. "Then where were you last night?"

She dropped her wet hands at her sides, too surprised to speak.

"I came by your hotel and you weren't there," he explained.

"I didn't know that. Did you leave a message?"

"No. I wanted to talk to you."

Kyla couldn't have been more surprised if the Dalai Lama had dropped by to talk to her.

"I'll be there tonight," she offered. Her curiosity overcame her desire to tell him he couldn't control her nighttime activities, too.

"About eight?"

She nodded. Any other person alone in a big, foreign city would have suggested dinner. But this man was not like everyone else, and she couldn't imagine what he wanted to talk to her about. Unless it was Lillian. But why couldn't they talk about her here?

As they dried their hands Chase told her about the patient who was waiting for them. A Tibetan refugee from nearby Patan, the old man had lost most of his family on a three-year flight from the invading Chinese army, and he himself had lost his sight. In spite of that, he ran a carpet shop, overseeing a dozen weavers with the help of his wife and elder son.

The surgery went smoothly, with Chase pointing to the instrument he needed, at the same time telling her what it was called. But she sensed his impatience when she hesitated, and she tried to work faster. She began concentrating on his hands, admiring his sure touch. It was better than looking him in the eye, because each time she did, she had a harder time looking away.

They did three more operations and at noon he dismissed her without saying anything more about meeting her that night. She hurried off to find lunch for Lillian.

That evening Kyla told herself to eat something while she waited for Chase to show up, but her stomach churned with unexpected nervousness. She felt as if she were waiting for a first date, when all it was was a medical discussion of some sort. The evenings were balmy in October in Kathmandu and Kyla dressed carefully in a handwoven peasant skirt dyed a brilliant red, and a pale pink silk blouse that matched the color of her cheeks.

Disgusted with her vanity, she shook her head at her reflection in the bathroom mirror and went to look in her duffel bag for a pair of jeans. There was a knock on the door. She threw the bag back into the closet and went to the door.

Chase seemed taller and broader in his casual linen jacket. And seeing his whole face without the usual green mask was a shock. She'd forgotten about the cleft in his chin and the lower lip that jutted out.

He seemed to have forgotten what she looked like, too. His eyes roamed over her from her leather sandals to her curly hair. Neither of them spoke for a long moment. Finally he broke the silence. "I thought we'd eat at the Vasera Hotel, if you don't mind going out of town."

"Eat? Eat dinner?"

"Yes, why? Have you already eaten?"

"No, but you never said... You said you wanted to talk to me."

"We can talk there. It's not a tourist place, though."

She heard the approval in his voice.

"That's fine with me," she assured him and followed him out. "What have you got against tourists?" she asked while they stood on the curb waiting for the taxi.

He didn't answer until they were hurtling through the crowded streets on their way across the river to Swayambula.

"Look around you and you'll see what the tourists have done to Kathmandu—the traffic, the noise, the smog. Imagine what the valley looked like fifty years ago, or even twenty-five. Next year when the new airport is finished there won't be two hundred thousand tourists a year, there'll be God only knows."

"What about the money the trekkers bring in? Don't you think we help the economy? Who would buy the carpets and the carvings and the cloth?" She fingered her soft wool skirt and wedged herself into the corner of the back seat, as far away from Dr. Chase as possible.

"Sure, you buy things, but you pay more than the local people can, so the prices go up and that causes inflation." He crossed his long legs.

"Local people barter," she countered. "And what about all the porters who work for us and take their money back to their villages? Have you ever heard of the trickle-down theory?"

"Yes, of course." He clamped his lips together. "I didn't bring you all the way out here to argue about economics."

"What did you bring me out here for?" she asked impatiently as the taxi pulled up in front of the old Vasera Hotel. He was the one who had started the argument. Now he apparently wanted to stop it, but he didn't know how.

When they were seated in the grand dining room under a ceiling covered with elaborate paintings of golden Buddhas, a maitre d' in a turban bowed low over their table and took their order. Still her question remained unanswered. There were candles in holders on the walls and fresh flowers on every table. From somewhere behind her, gamelans and other stringed instruments made music that sounded like the winds off the Himalayas.

The table was small, too small. When she shifted to the right her knees touched Chase's; when she shifted to the left, her legs brushed his. There was nowhere to look but at him—at his hair that fell across his forehead. He was looking at her; she knew that, but she would not—could not—meet his eyes. What did he want with her?

He put his hands on the table, spreading his fingers on the white tablecloth. "I work for Project Help. It was started about ten years ago by some philanthropist friends of my family. That's how I heard about it. Their goal is to wipe out blindness in Nepal."

She nodded. Was he trying to make her feel small and selfish for not having a worthwhile goal?

"I want to thank you for your help. I really didn't have any right to ask you. But I was desperate, and you've made a difference... a big difference."

She felt unexpected warmth in his words, but she accepted his thanks for what it was and nothing more. So that was what this was all about: he was taking her to dinner to thank her. There was no reason for her heart to skip around the way it was.

"You're welcome," she replied briskly. "It wasn't as bad as I thought it would be."

"We make a good team," he remarked, looking deep into her eyes.

She felt her cheeks flush and she looked around at the musicians in the corner, desperate to break the eye contact.

"Cataracts account for about two-thirds of the blindness in Nepal." He paused as the waiter set hearts-of-palm salad in front of them.

She picked up her fork, suddenly let down. This dinner had nothing to do with her as a person; it had to do with Kyla Tanner, the helpful assistant. "What about the other one-third?" she asked.

"It's a mix, mostly corneal infections. What accounts for only one percent is something called xerophthalmia, and that's what worries me the most."

"Why, if it's only one percent?"

"Because it affects children under the age of six. So if you count the actual number of years of blindness, it weighs much more heavily." He spoke dispassionately, but the lines in his forehead deepened.

"I've never seen any children in your hospital," she observed.

"No, because there's no cure for it. But the good thing is that it's easily prevented, with vitamins or green vegetables."

He paused again and she waited expectantly. What could this possibly have to do with her? Or was he just making conversation?

"Green vegetables aren't always available. But vitamins are. I want to take vitamin-A tablets up into the remote regions where the disease is epidemic. Have you ever been to the Manang Valley?"

"Yes, I led a tour there once. It's beautiful. It's walled in by Annapurna and the Glacier Dome." She set her fork down and gazed off in the distance, remembering villages of stone houses.

"What route did you take?" He leaned forward, his eyes bright and locked with hers.

"Through the valley of the Marysandi River. But it's a twenty-four-day trek back and forth. At least it was when I took my group."

"That's what I heard. The hospital has a guide lined up for me. We're planning to leave in a few weeks. It wasn't easy to find somebody. It's festival time and everyone wants to be at home, but finally I think it's going to work out."

Kyla watched a smile transform his face, making her smile back. "That's wonderful."

"So when you're paddling down—where is it?—the Yangtze River, I'll be climbing over some snow-covered pass." He took a drink of wine and set his glass down. "Here I am, spilling my guts about my obsession, and you've hardly said anything. What do you want to do with your life?"

She was afraid he was going to ask something like that. No matter what she told him, it would sound insignificant compared to preventing blindness in children. She couldn't say she was trying to beat the clock, to cram a lifetime of living into the years that she had left if... if...

"Me? I'm always looking for the next adventure. The one that makes my knees knock and my heart pound. But I don't make big plans for the future." She paused when the waiter brought their rich, creamy soup, and she took a sip. "It's a good thing I don't, or I'd be frustrated at having to hang around Kathmandu all this time. As it is..."

"As it is, you're restless and impatient," he said with a smile. But she heard the mild criticism in his voice.

"Does it show?" she asked carefully.

He answered with a question: "What's so bad about Kathmandu?"

"Just what you said: it's crowded and polluted and noisy. But once you start climbing and get up into the high country and the fresh air—" She broke off, realizing that that was just what he was going to do.

"But it's a fascinating city. It's a crossroads. Everybody and everything meets here. Have you seen the Nyatapola Temple?"

"No, I haven't. I've never spent much time in town before."

"What about Shiva or the Royal Palace?"

"No."

"The pagodas with the erotic carvings?"

"No."

Chase shook his head in mock despair. "You ought to see some of these things while you're stuck here."

She nodded. "I suppose so." But she had no intention of playing tourist.

"I can recommend a good guide." He smiled modestly. "Me."

"Oh, no," she protested. "You're much too busy. I couldn't let you."

"Yes, you could. Of course, I'm not in your league. Your group said you're the best guide in the Himalayas."

"You didn't believe all that, did you? All trekkers feel that way about their leader after a trip. They're caught up in the afterglow of a once-in-a-lifetime experience. They think you're wonderful. They even fall in love with you a little bit. They only remember the good parts. They forget that you made them walk that extra mile and sleep with the sheep."

"Well, I couldn't do anything like that."

"Like sleeping with the sheep?"

"Like falling in love with the guide."

Her mouth tilted upward and Chase watched with fascination as her color rose and her cheeks turned pink. Get hold of yourself, Cunningham. Quit looking at her like that. You brought her to thank her for helping you—just an ordinary gesture out of ordinary courtesy. But what he was feeling now was not at all ordinary. At least not for him.

"I didn't mean that you would," she protested.

"Because women don't understand about doctors," he continued.

"That their work comes first? I should think it would be obvious." She shifted in her chair and her knees brushed against his again. He felt a current of energy leap between them and he gripped the edge of the table.

"Well," she concluded briskly. "It's been a lovely dinner."

Was it possible that she didn't feel it? That she didn't notice that he was staring at her and saying anything that came into his head?

"I have to be up early tomorrow," she explained, "to get to work on time."

He rested his hand lightly on her back as they walked out of the dining room. "Your boss must be some kind of tyrant."

She slanted an appraising glance up at him as if trying to decide. "Let's say he's a very determined man."

Chase told himself to back off, and not insist on showing her around town. He should give her time to get to know him, to see that he wasn't a tyrant, that he had some redeeming traits. So on the way home he sat on his side of the taxi and she sat on hers and he talked about the cases he had lined up for the next day.

When he walked her into the hotel lobby she wore a remote look on her face that made him realize how little he knew her. He couldn't even guess what went on behind that smooth forehead. He imagined her miles away already, halfway to China, while he was still here waiting in the valley. And that made him feel hollow inside.

Chapter Three

By morning Kyla had Chase all figured out. He was a fanatic with a mission, who would let nothing stop him from fulfilling his destiny, which was wiping out blindness in Nepal; an attractive man with a noble purpose. Kyla had no intention of getting involved with either one.

Certainly his mission was worthwhile, but Kyla had her own dreams. The most pressing one was to get out of Kathmandu and on with her life. She was still thinking about his offer to be her guide around Kathmandu as she stood scrubbing before surgery promptly at six-thirty, and wondering how to discourage him if he brought it up again.

Chase didn't say much until they'd finished at noon. He caught up with her as she made her way toward the women's ward.

"Mr. Wangchen wants to see you."

"Who?"

"The old Tibetan refugee I operated on the second day you were here. He's leaving today and he wants to thank you."

She reluctantly followed him out into the courtyard. The small man with the round face and high cheekbones came forward from the crowd of people around him and clasped his hands together in the traditional greeting.

Kyla pressed her own hands together and murmured, "Namaste." It meant "I salute the goodness within you."

Mr. Wangchen turned to his teenage son next to him and spoke in rapid Tibetan. The son smiled shyly at Kyla. "My father wishes to invite you and his doctor to our home on Saturday."

Kyla shot Chase an inquiring look. He shrugged as if it didn't matter whether she accepted or not. "I think it would be interesting for you to see how the refugees live and how they make their carpets," he suggested, however.

"Yes, all right." She turned back to the son. "I'd be happy to come."

The son translated her answer and the group smiled and chattered with each other.

Chase opened the back door to the hospital for Kyla. "They live in Patan. It would be a shame not to see one of the most beautiful Buddhist monasteries in Nepal."

"I can't let you show me around the valley," she insisted. As she headed down the hall toward Lillian's ward, Chase walked along with her.

"One monastery isn't the valley," he replied mildly.

Kyla didn't answer. She was beginning to feel helplessly swept along by Chase's strong will. One way or another, it seemed that he was going to be her guide to the sights of Kathmandu.

"Is the monastery on our way?" she asked, although she already knew what the answer would be.

He nodded. "I'll pick you up at ten, Saturday morning."

Kyla wanted to say that was much too early, but a patient in a wheelchair caught her eye. The woman's arms moved spasmodically and her head jerked back and forth. She was trying to speak, but the words were garbled. Chase bent over to listen to her, and Kyla's blood ran cold. Wanting to run away, she felt rooted to the spot, unable to do anything but stand and stare. It was a horrible sight, one she hoped she would never have to see again.

Chase glanced up at her and his eyes widened in alarm when he saw the expression on her face. "What is it?"

Kyla's voice was barely a whisper. "What's wrong with her?"

"I don't know. She's not my patient." He stood and pressed his palm against Kyla's cheek, his thumb under her chin. "Are you all right?"

His fingers were cool and comforting. "Fine," she managed to say with stiff lips. Then, with great effort she drew back and found her way to Lillian's bed.

She got through the afternoon somehow. She brought Lillian her lunch and did some shopping for her. Together they wrote postcards to send home. Kyla's hands finally stopped shaking and Lillian didn't seem to notice that her attention wandered.

Of course it might not have been Huntington's that the woman had, but the symptoms were the same. Symptoms she knew so well they were engraved in her mind. Symptoms she feared so much they were part of an ongoing nightmare—the jerking, tripping, stumbling on words at the beginning; and at the end, a total inability to control the body.

She didn't see the woman in the wheelchair again, but she was never far out of her thoughts. By Saturday Kyla was so desperate for something else to think about that she was relieved to see Chase at her door at ten in the morning. He was dressed in a striped shirt and a dark blue blazer that was frayed at the cuffs. With his usual assurance he strode into her room and sat down on the edge of the bed without being invited. In spite of his casual pose, he seemed full of restless energy and his eyes challenged her.

"What do you know about Huntington's disease?" he asked.

Kyla drew a quick breath and stiffened. "Nothing. Why?"

"Because that's what the woman in the wheelchair has."

She shook her head. "I didn't know that."

He stared at her for a long moment, and she felt her face flame under his scrutiny. Chase walked over to her, put his hand on her shoulder and turned her toward him, forcing her to look into his eyes.

"I've been looking forward to getting away from the hospital, to seeing something besides the inside of the operating room. But if you're upset, if you don't want to go..."

Kyla's pulse raced. She suddenly realized how much she, too, needed to get away from the hospital, and how hard it was to admit it. When she didn't say anything, Chase abruptly dropped his hand and reached for the doorknob.

"Let's go."

Out on the street a brisk wind blew Kyla's hair into her face. Gray clouds hung over the distant peaks, and the air seemed as if it had been sucked clean of smoke and fumes.

"I thought the monsoon season was over." Kyla gratefully changed the subject to the weather and inhaled the smog-free air.

"It should be." Chase put his hand under her elbow and led her to the car he had waiting at the curb. "But the driver tells me the earth and water spirits are calling for thunder and rainbows."

He opened the door and followed her in. But instead of sitting in his corner, he sat in the middle, with his arm draped casually across the back of the seat. Kyla leaned forward to avoid his touch, and opened the window.

If only Chase had been a different kind of doctor, a kindly old family practitioner with gray hair and a comforting bedside manner, she might have been tempted to confide in him. But he had all the bedside manner of a tiger on the prowl, and there was no way she would ever let him see what drove her to live her life as she did. No one would ever know the fear she lived with. No one.

She crossed and uncrossed her bare legs, each time brushing against the khaki pants he wore, and feeling the electricity crackle in the air. It might have been "the spirits" at work, but she knew it wasn't. She wished she had suggested walking instead of riding across the river to Patan.

Chase seemed to feel the changes in the atmosphere, too. He spoke to the driver, who pulled over to let them out at the bridge. Kyla leaned over the railing to look into the muddy waters that were sacred to the Hindus. Although her hair was tangled from the wind, she was glad to see that her mirrored face below didn't reveal any of the turmoil she was feeling.

Her gaze met Chase's in the reflection. There was a probing look in his eyes that disturbed her, but it wasn't pity, and that was what she would have seen if she had told him about her familiarity with the disease. She picked up a stone and threw it down, distorting the image of their reflected faces in the water.

"Are we going to the monastery?" she asked.

"We are," he answered, taking her hand in his, gently pressing his thumb against her palm.

It was a good thing he wasn't taking her pulse, or he would have felt it throbbing. With an effort she kept her voice even. "Then we should stop and buy a gift scarf for the high priest and put a donation in it—some tea or something."

"Good idea." Traffic raced past them on one side, while brown water flowed by on the other. "Are you going to receive his blessing, or ask him about your Karma?"

She shook her head and pulled her hand away. "I don't want to know my fate. My future will take care of itself. But you go right ahead."

He nodded and they walked across the bridge to the city gate and the gift shop.

"Don't you believe in reincarnation?" he asked while she sifted through a stack of scarves.

She looked up to see him leaning against a rack of souvenir bronze Buddhas, a half smile on his face. "Do you?" she questioned.

He folded his arms across his chest. "Sometimes. Sometimes I have the feeling I've lived another life somewhere. When I first came to Nepal I had a sense of coming home. Do you know what I mean?"

She shook her head and paid for a scarf and a box of tea. "I don't really have a home. I mostly live out of a suitcase."

Behind the shop they followed a narrow alleyway lined with handicraft shops. They walked side by side, shoulders touching. "What about your parents?" Chase watched Kyla's face out of the corner of his eye. He saw her mouth tighten, watched her brush her lips with the back of her hand.

"My mother died a few years ago, and my father's remarried. She's a nice person, but the house doesn't feel like home anymore. My mother's family has a house on Puget Sound, but..." She paused in front of a rack of brass bells for sale. "I don't know why I'm telling you all this."

"I asked you," he reminded her.

"Oh, yes." She looked around as if he'd trapped her, and Chase berated himself for coming up with too many questions. It was obvious she was a private person, even to the members of her group who idolized her without really knowing her. "Where is that monastery?" she asked pointedly.

He gestured toward the square and she set off ahead of him, just far enough that he could admire the set of her shoulders, the spring in her step and the curve of her hips. He was determined to get to know her. As for idolizing her, what he felt for her was much more earthy.

Shoppers separated them and Chase didn't catch up with her until he reached the courtyard of the twelfth-century monastery. She had presented her gift to the high priest and was staring up at the scenes painted on the walls of the life of Buddha, her face composed and serene. He had upset her; Buddha had calmed her down. From now on, he'd wait until she volunteered information.

He leaned over to whisper in her ear. "The gold-plated roof was donated by a rich merchant."

They looked up and shaded their eyes from the glare. Then they walked slowly around the courtyard examining the hand-carved prayer wheels. Back in the square, Chase debated about showing her the erotic carvings on the Jagannath Temple. Still, in the interests of architecture and history, he decided he owed it to her. He led the way.

She tilted her head for a better view of naked bodies with their limbs wrapped around each other, and avoided his gaze. He realized that her eyes were the color of the sky today and just as changeable. When he caught her eye she blushed.

"They don't seem . . ." She paused, unwilling to let him know how inexperienced she was. "They don't seem anatomically correct." She backed away from him to review the carvings as if she saw such scenes every day.

"Not really," he agreed. "I admire them more as objects of art."

"Of course," she replied. "But I'm surprised they'd put them on temples, given the subject matter."

"I can explain that." He looked up at the gray clouds racing across the sky. "The goddess of lightning is a chaste virgin and she would never consider striking a temple with such shocking goings-on."

She followed his gaze. "It feels as if she might be looking for someplace to strike today."

"We'll have to hurry if we want to get to the Wangchens' before the storm."

They made their way past traders' camps where horses were tethered beside yak-hair tents, past shops selling mystic stones and Chinese sneakers. Finally they reached a row of new shops. The one in the middle had piles of carpets on the floor and more hanging on the walls. Mr. Wangchen's son rose from behind a small desk in the corner and greeted them with an ear-splitting grin on his face.

"Welcome to my father's doctor and to his lady."

Chase tried to ignore the startled look on Kyla's face. He didn't know who they thought she was, except perhaps a nurse.

The Wangchen son led them up a narrow flight of stairs to the living quarters above the store.

"What have you told them about me?" Kyla muttered over her shoulder.

"Nothing," he insisted under his breath. "I don't know where they got this 'my lady' idea."

Mr. Wangchen, his wife and their younger son stood at attention as they entered the large carpeted living room as honored guests. They shook hands and then sat on a sofa in front of an intricately carved rosewood table. Mrs. Wangchen left to bring the tea, and the older son translated his father's gratitude.

"The government of Nepal has given our family many things," he began. "Most of all they have given us freedom—to work, to travel and to receive excellent medical care."

Chase lowered his head as a sign of humility, and the son continued. "At your hospital we have not only received such care but also such attention and . . . and—" he wrinkled his nose as he searched for the word "—kindness. For three long years my father knew only hardship and deprivation. That time has faded like a bad dream."

Mr. Wangchen nodded and a tear slid down his cheek. Kyla was holding her head stiffly. "Now the final wrong has been righted. You have restored his sight to him." He held his hands together. "We thank you . . . both."

Mrs. Wangchen appeared with the tea, her face wreathed in smiles, and Mr. Wangchen brought forward an exquisite finely woven silk carpet in shades of blue and silver. He stretched it across Kyla's and Chase's knees. She looked up at Chase, her eyes wide and imploring.

"I don't know what to say," she whispered.

"Say thank-you."

"It's not for me. I can't accept it. It's yours."

He shook his head. "It's ours. It's for both of us."

"There is no 'us,'" she whispered urgently. "Somehow they've gotten the wrong idea."

Mr. Wangchen rubbed his forehead and spoke to his son.

"My father asks is there something wrong? You do not like the carpet?"

"It is beautiful," Kyla assured him. "We like it very much."

"We'll treasure it forever," Chase said emphatically, looking at Kyla.

After tea and cakes and more thank-yous, Chase and Kyla followed their host down the stairs and out onto the street. Again the tears came to Mr. Wangchen's eyes when he said goodbye.

"I never forget you," he told Chase, and Chase coughed to dislodge the lump in his throat as they walked away.

They stopped at a café in Durbar Square and sat at an outside table under an awning, putting the folded carpet on a third chair. A few drops of rain hit the sidewalk and Chase pulled Kyla's chair closer to him.

"Do you want to go inside?" His voice sounded too loud in the hush before the electrical storm.

She shook her head. "I like it out here."

Chase, too, liked the air charged with electricity. He liked having Kyla next to him, and felt as if they were the only two people at the café, the only people in the square—the only people in the world.

Kyla slid her chair away from him, and the sound of metal against cement grated on his nerves. "What was that all about back there?" she demanded.

"I told you I don't know. He knows you assisted at the operation. He's seen you in the hospital. I imagine most patients think you're a nurse, not my...my...anything." His forehead wrinkled and he took a sip of cold Chinese beer. "Oh, my God."

Kyla leaned forward. "What is it?"

"I think I understand." He leaned back in his chair and exhaled slowly. "Mr. Wangchen was one of my first patients when I arrived a year and a half ago. It was too soon to operate on his cataract, so I gave him another appointment. But he was curious. He asked me why I wasn't married at my age, and I told him I had a fiancée."

Kyla's eyes shifted to the gray sky, her expression showing more interest in the weather than in his explanation. If he thought she cared whether he had a fiancée or not, he was mistaken.

"I told him she would be joining me later, and since you're the only American woman on the scene, he assumes you're her." He set his beer down. "That must be it."

"That must be it," she echoed in small, tight voice. There was a long silence while he waited for her to say something else, maybe ask whatever happened to his fiancée. But she didn't.

"You're probably wondering if I really had a fiancée," he finally prompted.

He was rewarded by a small smile tugging at the corner of her mouth. "Did you really have a fiancée?" she asked dutifully.

"Yes, but she never joined me. Once I got here I knew she wouldn't like it."

Kyla looked at him curiously. "Even though you felt at home here?"

"Yeah. It's funny, isn't it? Coming here changed my life. I planned to stay a few months—a year at the most—but once I saw the valley and met the people and saw what had to be done...I don't know. I just knew nothing else was as important."

"Even your fiancée?"

"Yes." He spread his hands on the table. "It sounds heartless, maybe, but I was doing her a favor. She wouldn't have lasted two days here." He didn't say that Kristie had refused to join him; that she'd wanted to marry a doctor, not a do-gooder. He didn't say how lonely he'd felt at first, how deserted. It wasn't important. It was a long time ago, and time had healed the wounds . . . almost.

He stood and held his hands out. "Let's get you and your carpet home before the storm comes."

She sighed. "It's not my carpet, it's yours. I don't have room for a carpet, I don't have room for a rabbit's foot. Please."

"All right. I'll keep it for you until you have room. Until you have your own home." He knew as soon as he'd said it that it was the wrong thing to say. Her eyes, which had shone warmly, now glinted like steel.

On the way back, she quickened her pace as if she couldn't stand to spend another minute with him. He'd stepped over some invisible barrier she'd set up, and she'd become the intrepid tour guide again, striding ahead to the campsite.

At the hotel she mumbled something polite and ran up the steps, leaving him with the carpet under his arm and the long-awaited rain falling on his head. He walked home slowly, not noticing that the downpour had soaked his blazer and shirt. He tried to understand what made her tick, but he couldn't. What drove her to climb the highest peak and swim the deepest ocean, to give up having a home and family? Was she really the thrill seeker she claimed to be? What was she hiding from him?

Whatever it was, he wasn't going to find out easily. She had a way of shutting him out so quickly and so unexpectedly. Let her go, he told himself. You've got to get back to work. Soon he'd be on his way to the Manang Valley, fulfilling his own dream at last. And Kyla Tanner would be in China, doing what she wanted to do. It would be as if this brief episode had never happened and they had never met. He was soaked to the skin now; his wet clothes made him feel cold and clammy. And the thought of never seeing her again made the chill penetrate all the way to his heart.

Chapter Four

The earth and water spirits continued to call for thunder and rainbows during the next few days, but what came instead was a warm, dull rain. Kyla was pleased that the dust no longer swirled in front of the hospital, but that was about all she had to be grateful for. Mr. Wangchen and his formal thank-you speech had made her feel small and self-centered for not doing more to help sick people.

In her dreams she saw blind children who called out to her to help them, but she turned and walked away and went to test the rapids on the Yangtze River.

Chase made no more mention of his trip to the Manang Valley. He didn't offer to show her any more temples or palaces or monasteries, either. They only talked about the patients, and the days dragged by. The nights dragged, too. In the long evenings, there was no one to talk to, and in her sleep she tossed and turned, thinking about the children who needed vitamin A.

On Friday morning in surgery, Chase dropped the scissors Kyla handed him. They clattered to the floor and Kyla raised her eyebrows in surprise. He jabbed his finger at a drawer full of sterilized instruments, and she reached for another pair and handed them to him. He stared at her for a long moment, then turned back to the patient, cutting and stitching as if nothing had happened. The look in his dark eyes told her something was wrong, but she could see from the way he worked, he wasn't going to let it affect him.

When they finished, he didn't wait for her to discuss the patient as he usually did. Instead he stripped off his green gown, pushed the swing doors open and strode down the hall.

Kyla followed him. "What's wrong?" she asked as he rounded the corner.

He turned and glared at her. "I dropped the scissors, that's all. I've never done it before, and I'll probably never do it again. It's nothing to worry about."

His face showed the fatigue of the long hours he spent working, the painstaking care he took with the hundreds of patients he saw. She wanted to smooth the lines around his mouth and the creases in his forehead. But she simply put her hand on his arm.

"I'm worried. When was the last time you took a day off?" As soon as she asked, she knew the answer. It was the day they went to the Wangchens', the day that started off with the promise of rainbows and ended in a drenching shower that neither one of them had recovered from.

"You look tired," she observed.

"It's the weather," he apologized. "I've got meteorological depression syndrome."

She tilted her head to one side and gazed up at him. "Is there any known cure?"

He looked at her for a long moment as if he were trying to make up his mind about something. "Some sunshine, for a change. Maybe even a rainbow. A whole day up out of this valley."

"Where?" she asked.

"A place I know. Would you like to come along?"

"When?" she asked, feeling herself swept along again by Chase and doing what he wanted to do.

"Tomorrow."

She sighed, half relieved, half disappointed. "I can't. I have Lillian."

"One of the nurses came back last night. I'll ask her to look in on Lillian, bring her meals." He spoke as if it were all decided, as if he'd already arranged it. Maybe he had.

She fought the feeling of lighthearted exuberance at the thought of a day away from the hospital, a day with Chase. "Are you sure?"

"Yes. But you have to promise not to talk about the past or the future. Or the cure won't take, and my syndrome will come back."

"You mean you won't talk about the Manang Valley, either?" she asked dubiously.

"Definitely not the Manang Valley," he promised emphatically. Then he told her to bring a raincoat just in case and to be ready at dawn. He added that they'd have to take a bus.

She returned to the hotel, telling herself not to get so excited. It was just a day off with a little sightseeing—a casual excursion. But it was a funny feeling, not being in charge, not knowing where she was going. It was also scary, because she liked being in control.

Ever since the day she'd walked into Chase's hospital her schedule had been disrupted and she'd felt a recurring panic that surfaced unexpectedly. It was caused partly by the helplessness of being stuck and not knowing exactly when she could leave. But it was really Chase himself, the most disturbing man she'd ever met. She'd met attractive men before. They were on her tours and they sometimes made passes at her. But there were rules about guides and trekkers, and Kyla had her own rules that were stricter than any Adventure Travel could ever have thought up. No affairs, because for Kyla, sex meant more than physical attraction, and emotional was out of the question. But she had to admit she'd never been tempted so strongly before.

She lay awake most of that night, afraid if she fell asleep she'd dream about Chase; afraid she shouldn't go anywhere with Chase, even for a day, even for an hour. There was something about him that touched her deep down where she'd never been touched before.

She finally fell asleep, but almost immediately there was a knock at the door. She staggered across the room and opened the door a crack.

"You're not ready," he accused, glancing briefly at the white cotton nightgown that grazed her knees.

She squinted at him. "Are you sure it's dawn? It seems like the middle of the night."

He nodded. "I'll wait for you downstairs."

He paced back and forth in the deserted lobby. He should have had the hotel clerk phone up to tell her he was there. He didn't need to see her hair in a tangle, her gray eyes heavy with sleep, the outline of her breasts under the nightgown. He was already thinking about her more than was reasonable, and more than he'd thought possible.

He didn't need to catch her unawares. She had looked vulnerable and so desirable he'd almost pushed the door open and taken her in his arms.

It was time to let Kyla Tanner go. It wasn't fair to her to hold on to her any longer, and he would tell her so today.

She wouldn't even have to go back to the hospital except to say goodbye to Lillian. She might never have to be with him again.

He saw her walking across the lobby in khaki pants, a vivid purple shirt and a khaki jacket, looking like some tropical bird, and his heart pounded in his chest. Never have to be with him again. *Never.* That was a long time.

She smiled tentatively, her gray eyes reflecting lights from the old-fashioned chandeliers. He nodded approvingly at her backpack. "You look like you're ready for anything."

But was he? Yes, he was ready for anything but saying goodbye to her.

They caught a taxi, rode to the edge of town, then got out to wait for the bus. Kyla looked around curiously at laughing, smiling Newars loaded down with ducks in wicker cages. When the bus came, she and Chase boarded and found themselves wedged between farmers holding bulging bags of rice and women in shawls and black skirts above tattooed ankles.

Her hip rubbed against Chase's. He rested his arm on the back of the seat and brushed her neck. She turned to look out the window, afraid to meet his eyes. The bus was climbing, leaving the valley behind, and she felt the tingle of excitement she always did at the beginning of a trip. Never mind that it was only for one day. The tingling had nothing to do with Chase, she assured herself; nothing to do with the fact that when the road curved she felt his arm tighten around her shoulders, or that they were so close she could feel his warm breath on her cheek.

The dirt road ended, the passengers all got out, and it started to rain. Kyla unzipped her backpack and took out her raincoat; Chase pulled an orange anorak over his head. They cut through rice fields. Kyla's skin began to stick to her clothes, and perspiration mingled with rain and dripped down her forehead.

Chase stopped at the edge of a field; the rain was falling off his hood onto his eyelashes. "I'm sorry about this."

She shook her head. "It doesn't matter. It's good to be out of town, to be walking again. Where are we going?"

He pointed up past women cutting rice stalks on hillside terraces. "That way."

A half hour later the rain stopped and they paused to stow away their rain gear.

"Does it have a name?" Kyla asked. She was used to being the leader. She was even used to the constant questions—"How much longer will it take? How many more miles? Where's the best place to take a picture? What are we having for lunch?" But she was not used to being kept in the dark.

"Yes," he answered, and she bit her lip to keep from protesting.

They were following a narrow road that became an uneven dirt driveway, and she found the answer to her question carved on a simple wooden sign: Himalayan View Hotel. She didn't know what she had expected, but it wasn't this innocuous two-story brick building. She walked ahead of Chase so he couldn't see the disappointment on her face.

The stone walkway led to a terrace and suddenly Kyla stood among red cannas and yellow marigolds blooming with dazzling color. She held her breath for a long moment. There above the hills shining emerald green in the brilliant sunlight, rose the white peak of Mount Everest.

She let the pack slide off of her back and Chase caught it. She inhaled the fresh clean air. "This is heaven," she breathed softly.

He looked up at Everest. "No. That's heaven up there. We're only halfway."

She smiled. Birds floated on the wind from the valley below, and from somewhere came flute music, plaintive and sweet. Suddenly light-headed, she sat down in a woven chaise longue.

Chase put his hand on her shoulder. "You haven't had breakfast. I'll go in and get us something to eat."

Because she was speechless, she reached for his hand to show him how much she liked this place. But he was gone, and she knotted her hands together in her lap.

When he came back, he was followed by a thin, smiling waiter carrying a tray of covered dishes. They turned out to be crisp *somozas* stuffed with spinach and sweet potato, and dahl with rice and lamb curry in a rich, brown sauce.

Kyla looked up, wide-eyed. "Is this breakfast?"

"It's food," he explained. "And they'll keep bringing it until we tell them to stop."

"Stop," she said, holding her hand up. "There are only two of us."

Chase lowered himself into the chair next to hers and looked around at the empty terrace and the empty valley below. "Thank God," he muttered under his breath.

Kyla ate more than she'd eaten in the past week, suddenly ravenous from the altitude and the exercise. Then they sipped sweet, hot coffee, and she leaned back in her chair and closed her eyes. She moved only to take off her jacket and shoes, then let the sun warm her.

She felt as if she were floating over the valley with the hawks, and she slept—deeply, peacefully, as if she didn't have a worry in the world. When she woke up there were shadows across the valley and Chase was watching her from the edge of the terrace where he was leaning against the wooden railing.

"I could stay here forever," she murmured sleepily.

"How about overnight?" he asked impulsively.

She looked around at the screenless windows of the rooms that opened out to the view. Then her gaze swiveled back to his. There was an intensity in his eyes that held her, and she swallowed hard.

"I don't think so."

"Forever starts now," he said.

"Not for me."

"Kyla..."

She jumped. There was urgency in his voice.

"The nurse who's taking care of Lillian today will stay on so you can leave. She's back from her holiday, and she's willing to take over for you if you want her. She speaks English and I think Lillian will like her."

She stood and stared at him. "You mean I can go to China?" Then she remembered their agreement and she clamped her hand over her mouth.

The corners of his mouth turned up, but his eyes were dark and somber. "Go ahead and talk about it. I know how much it means to you. I'm sorry I couldn't arrange it sooner."

"Then I'm free." She didn't know whether to laugh or cry, so she stood and threw her arms around Chase and was instantly sorry she had. The sun-dried smell of his shirt, the pure air and the physical contact with his chest unleashed a flood of pent-up desire within her and made her pull back in alarm.

He folded his arms and looked at her. If he knew the effect he had on her, he didn't let on. She propped her elbows on the railing to steady herself, and watched the fog obscure the tops of the white mountains. Somewhere behind the range was the Manang Valley. Somewhere there were children waiting for help. If they didn't get it they would go blind. She cleared her throat.

"What about you? When do you leave on your trek?"

He hesitated. "I'm not sure. Not this fall, probably. There's some problem with the guide. The one we had can't make it, and no one else wants to go during the holiday season."

The words were casual, but Kyla heard the disappointment in his voice and saw it in his eyes. "When did you find out? You never told me you weren't going."

"I just heard yesterday."

"Before surgery." The dropped instrument, the sudden depression were suddenly explained.

"Yes," he admitted. "It's probably better to wait until spring, anyway. The passes will be blocked with snow soon."

"You could still make it, if you had a guide."

"I don't have one."

"But if you did," she insisted, knowing that if he asked her now, she would say yes.

He shook his head. "Don't worry about it. It's not your problem."

"It's not yours, either, but you're going. You need a guide. *I*'m a guide. Maybe it's fate. Maybe I'm destined to go with you."

"I thought you didn't believe in destiny."

Damn it, she thought. Was she going to have to beg him to let her take him? Maybe he didn't want her along, but right now he didn't have a choice.

She took a deep breath. "If you want me to take you I will." There, she'd said it. Now it was up to him.

The sun was setting behind the mountains, and his face was in shadow. "What about China?" he asked.

"They found somebody to take my place, so I'm free. I'll go some other time." Her voice sounded cool and calm in her ears, but inside she was shaking. Why was she doing this? Practically pleading with him to take her with him when she could pick up the pieces of her life by getting out of Nepal right away. Was it because this was a chance to make her life meaningful by doing something for somebody else? Was it because of the children? Or was it Chase himself? Was it an unconscious desire to see more of him, to find out what went on underneath the green surgeon's mask? If it was—if she was going on a twenty-four-day trip just to be with a man she was attracted to—she'd better get on the first plane to China.

He pulled her away from the railing and held her by the shoulders. "Are you sure about this?" His eyes questioned her, probed her for motives.

"Yes." She tried to look away, but she couldn't. "I . . . I owe it to you, to the children."

The terrace was half in shadow now and Kyla shivered. What had she done? She had committed herself to a difficult trip with a difficult man.

"Let's get something to drink before we head back," Chase suggested, as if nothing very significant had happened.

Kyla took one more look at the open windows. How would it feel to wake up and see the sun rise on Everest? Chase followed her gaze but said nothing.

Inside, at the small wood-paneled bar, they sipped brandy and asked for the bus schedule. The turbaned bartender sighed.

"The bus is stuck in the mud, sir," he told Chase. "Tomorrow he will resume his schedule."

Kyla looked up from her drink, and Chase shrugged.

"We are not accustomed to rain this late in the season," the bar man apologized.

"I guess we'll take two rooms for tonight," Chase told him, and Kyla, warmed by the brandy, nodded. Lillian was cared for. What harm was there in spending the night in a place that was halfway to heaven?

The bartender stopped polishing glasses. "But we are full tonight."

They looked around the empty bar incredulously. "What?"

The man folded his towel on the counter and looked at them. "It is Colonel Prajapati and his group. They come every year. During the day they do the hiking, at night they have a comfortable stay here."

"The colonel runs a trekking operation in Kathmandu the way he used to run the army in India," Kyla informed Chase. "But he likes his gin and tonic at the end of the day."

At that very moment there were footsteps on the stone driveway and voices drifting through the evening air. In minutes the bar was filled with dusty hikers, exuberant after surviving a day in the mountains with Colonel Prajapati.

The colonel spotted Kyla and carried his frosty glass to their table. "A pleasure to see you, my dear Miss Kyla." He raised his glass to hers, and Kyla introduced Chase. "How did you manage, Doctor, to find not only the second-best guide in the Himalayas, but the most beautiful?"

Chase looked at Kyla's sunburned face, her dark lashes lowered against pink cheeks. The most beautiful, he thought, and the most intriguing and the least likely to ever let him see beyond her elaborate defense system.

"Just lucky, Colonel," Chase responded easily. "Tell me, are you using all twelve rooms tonight?"

Colonel Prajapati looked around the bar, counting heads. "I could perhaps prevail upon my hikers to double up and provide you with a room." His eyes traveled to Chase and then to Kyla, who was looking alarmed.

"Two," she said firmly.

"To help us out," Chase cut in.

"Of course. And since I have the large room on the end, I could accommodate one of you." His long look at Kyla made it clear which of them he meant.

Chase deliberately put his hand over Kyla's in full view of the colonel. "That won't be necessary. It was careless of us not to make reservations, but if you can spare us a room..."

The colonel stood and bowed and went to mingle with his group at the bar.

"What do you mean, 'That won't be necessary'?" Kyla muttered under her breath, and pulled her hand away. "Why can't you sleep with the colonel?"

"He doesn't want me, he wants you."

She folded her arms across her chest. "He can't have me."

He watched her grey eyes turn dark. "Can anyone?" he asked softly, and she shook her head.

The colonel came back with the key to the room above the terrace and pressed it into Kyla's palm. "Pleasant dreams," he told her with an elaborate wink.

"There goes your reputation," Chase said out of the corner of his mouth. "The ice princess melts."

Her throaty chuckle surprised him. He expected a reaction, but not that kind. He thought she might want to prove him wrong.

"Is that what you think?" Her eyes gleamed.

"I think you're only slightly repressed." His smile softened the words.

"That's your professional opinion," she replied lightly.

"It's just a hunch."

"Actually—" Kyla swirled the brandy around in her glass "—tour guides have a terrible reputation. They say we'll do anything to keep the campers happy."

He drained his glass. "Will you?"

"No."

A gong sounded and they stood and followed the boisterous trekkers into the dining room. Their laughter and good-natured banter lasted through the meal, after which Chase and Kyla silently went to their bedroom. It was small but it had a big view.

Chase leaned against the door and Kyla stepped out to the terrace to watch the moon rise over the mountain range. Even without the lights on he could see there was only one bed. His heart pounded. It could have been the altitude, but it wasn't. Why was she going with him to the Manang Valley? What had made her change her mind? He saw the outline of her body in the moonlight, the rise of her breast, the curve of her hip, her tender profile that took his breath away.

He took off his shoes and shoved them under the bed. On stocking feet he walked up behind her and ran his hands down her arms. She shivered but didn't pull away. He could smell the sunshine in her hair and he wanted to bury his head in the unruly curls that formed a halo around her head. The first day he saw her he'd wanted to touch her hair, to see if it felt the way it looked: soft and warm and alive.

She leaned back against him and he breathed hard, nuzzling her neck with his chin. Then she stiffened and turned around.

"Chase," she said in that throaty, husky voice that made him feel as if he had fire in his veins. "We have to have some kind of understanding."

"Yes, fine," he answered quickly, ready to agree to anything.

"Not just for tonight, but for the whole trip," she explained. "I'm not going to sleep with you."

He took a deep breath and glanced at the double bed.

"I mean, I have to sleep with you, but I'm not going to sleep with you."

"I see," he said, listening to her voice as if it were music, but not understanding the words. A few seconds later the meaning sank in. Frustrated by not being able to read the expression on her face, he turned her by the shoulders until the moonlight shone on her. "Why not?"

"I make it a point not to get involved with anyone in my group."

"I'm not in your group," he pointed out.

"Or outside my group," she added.

"Kyla, you can't go through life without getting involved. It's not possible. Especially for someone as young and outgoing as you are. It's not healthy." He wanted to push her into telling him what he needed to know. What was she afraid of?

A tremor passed over her pale features. "You may be a doctor, but I know what's healthy for me and what isn't. And I'm not getting involved—with you or with anyone. Sexually or emotionally." She gripped his arms so tightly, he felt her fingernails through the rough fabric of his shirt.

Her eyes shone with unshed tears and Chase put his arms around her gently, knowing that she couldn't be held by force. She rested her forehead against his chest and he was afraid to breathe. There was no sound but a light rain blowing across the fields below.

When she looked up, her eyes were dry and a slight smile hovered on her lips. "Well, now that we have that settled, let's go to sleep."

"In the same bed?" he asked incredulously.

"Do you see another one?" she asked.

He shook his head in amazement. Maybe she didn't feel the way he did. Maybe she was going with him because she only wanted to do good for someone. That made things simpler. He didn't have to lie awake thinking about kissing her, wondering if her lips would taste like the wine they drank at dinner. Because now he would never know. She'd made that perfectly clear. No involvement.

Obviously she didn't feel anything for him at all, he realized seconds later as they lay on the bed. She'd fallen asleep right away, her body only inches from his. Feeling stupid, he turned over and stared out the window until the sun rose and lighted the white peaks with an orange glow. She was right. It was good to have these things settled early on, before they started the trip—before he'd made a complete fool of himself.

When she woke up he crossed his arms under his head on the pillow and watched her take her backpack and leave the room to go down the hall to the bathroom. She came back, her teeth gleaming, her face scrubbed and her hair combed. She looked as if she were ready for anything—anything, that is, except an emotional or sexual involvement. She looked beyond him out the window.

"Guess what?" she asked.

He stood, but his mouth was too dry for him to speak. His clothes felt glued to his skin. He ran his hand over the stubble on his chin. "What?" he croaked.

"There's a rainbow out there."

Barefoot, he stepped out onto the balcony. There were clouds and a pale sun, and a rainbow that stretched across the sky and ended somewhere behind Mount Everest.

He felt her hand on his shoulder, but he didn't move. "Thank you," she said softly. He nodded, unable to speak, unable to control the tension any longer. She might be made of ice, but he wasn't. He cleared his throat.

"For what?" he demanded harshly. "The rainbow or half of the bed? Or my admirable restraint in not ravishing you in your sleep?"

She dropped her hand from his shoulder as if she'd been burned. "Yes, all of the above. Shall we go?"

On the way down, Kyla sat in bewildered silence between a Tibetan woman in a bright sweater and Chase in his damp, wrinkled shirt. She thought she'd done the right thing, but had she? You laid out the rules at the beginning of the trip, and made sure everyone understood them. That way, they couldn't say they didn't know they weren't supposed to drink the water or sleep with the leader. And Chase had been a model camper until this morning. Why had he lashed out at her that way?

She left him at the bus stop in Kathmandu and stomped off toward her hotel in her mud-caked hiking boots. Refusing to look back to see if he was still staring at her, she wondered how she was going to survive twenty-four days with a man who didn't want to follow the rules.

She was still thinking the same thought when she made the rounds on Monday morning. She bought a stove and food supplies, rented a tent and sleeping bags and hired a Sherpa to be their porter. Then she went to the local Adventure Travel office, which was wedged between a tea shop and a store that sold hi-tech climbing equipment, to tell them about the trip. Finally she stopped by the hospital to say goodbye to Lillian.

The woman had tears in her eyes when Kyla announced her plans. "I know you're doing the right thing," she said, her lower lip trembling. "But I'll miss you. Dr. Chase says I can go home in a week or two. Where will you be then?"

Kyla heard voices approaching—Chase and another doctor making rounds. She reached up and closed the curtain around Lillian's bed.

"With any luck we'll be halfway there," she said, deliberately blocking out the sound of Chase's voice. If only she'd left a few minutes ago, she wouldn't have to face him until they met at the airport in the morning. Now, in order to avoid him, she'd have to stay with Lillian until he'd finished touring the whole ward.

Chase's voice was louder, closer. If she saw him she might tell him what she thought of him and his advice to get involved. She *was* involved—with life, with people—but not with him; and she never would be. She leaned against Lillian's bed, holding herself perfectly still, but Lillian heard Chase speak to the patient in the next bed.

"We're in here," she called loudly, and Kyla winced.

He threw back the curtain and stood there in a white coat, his arms crossed. She hadn't seen him since the bus stop. They had discussed preparations only by telephone, and she wasn't ready for his clean-shaven face, his hair falling across his forehead, or the gleam in his eyes.

Kyla gently hugged Lillian and told her she'd call her in the States. Then she ducked out and almost ran down the hall to the lobby. But Chase was right behind her.

"Where have you been? I came by last night. They said you were out."

"I *was* out. I was lining up a Sherpa to meet us at Pokhara."

"Then you haven't changed your mind?" Chase asked, matching her stride.

She shook her head. "I never change my mind."

"That's what I thought." Chase opened the front door for her and she hesitated, feeling his eyes on her.

"I didn't thank you for the . . . uh, the day in the mountains." She stared up the street, barely seeing the dust, the traffic and the throngs of people. "It's a beautiful place, and I felt like I was under a spell for a while." She looked up at him. So please understand, she wanted to say, that I can't let down my guard again.

"I got over my syndrome." His dark eyes crinkled at the corners.

She smiled. "And I got caught up on my sleep. It must have been the air or something." He was looking at her so intently it made her knees shake. Kyla, the fearless guide, afraid to take on one single do-gooder for twenty-four days? Of course not.

It was Chase who finally turned away to go back in. "I've got patients to see," he explained. "Last-minute charts to write."

"Are you sure you can be ready tomorrow?"

He nodded. "I'll see you at the airport at seven. Unless you change your mind."

"I don't—"

"I know you don't. I'm just very. . ." He paused, one hand on the door. "I'm just a little overwhelmed. I thought I'd never have a chance to reach those people. And now we're actually going. . .tomorrow." His smile started slowly and transformed his face. Kyla smiled back, catching the anticipation, the excitement and the wonder in his expression.

She waved at Chase with one hand and signaled for a taxi with the other. He looked like a kid going camping for the first time. *Was* he going camping for the first time? She had forgotten to ask. What kind of guide was she? She sighed. It didn't matter. She had promised to take him, and she never changed her mind.

Chapter Five

Next morning, they met at the airport as arranged, and stowed their luggage behind the two rows of seats in the tiny airplane.

"What's in there?" Kyla pointed to Chase's bulging canvas duffel bag.

He took the seat behind her and shouted into her ear over the roar of the twin engines. "I brought a few instruments and some supplies, the vitamin A and antibiotics."

Kyla shook her head. She never brought that much when she was on a trip around the world. "It looks like you brought your whole lab," she yelled over her shoulder.

He shrugged. "You never know what you'll need. I like to be prepared."

She turned around to face the cockpit and the plane taxied down the narrow runway. You never knew what would happen, either; and you couldn't possibly be prepared for everything, Kyla thought. That was what made these trips so exhilarating.

Her spirits lifted as the plane rose in the air. Beginnings were the best part, before the tired muscles and the light-headedness caused by the high altitudes set in. What kind of hiker would Chase turn out to be? More important, what kind of person would he turn out to be? She suddenly realized that she didn't know anything about his life before he came to Nepal.

Before she left on a regular trek she would study the application forms of the members of her group. Question number one: "Describe your outdoor background." It was too noisy in the plane to ask him to describe anything. The last time she'd seen him in an outdoor background, on the way down from the Himalayan View Hotel, he was walking faster than she was, leaving her trailing behind him in the dust. It wasn't a pleasant memory.

Next question: "In case of emergency, please notify..." If Chase fell and hurt his back the way Lillian had, she wouldn't have Adventure Travel to notify the next of kin. She would have to call his mother or father—or would it be his ex-fiancée? She frowned and mentally moved on to the next question: "State of health." She had already observed the broad shoulders, the muscle tone, the gleam in his eyes, the wide generous mouth. State of *health*? She was confusing good health with good looks.

Question four: "Accommodations—prefer single or double?" She blushed at the thought of the bed where she'd spent the night pretending to be asleep next to Chase. She had lain so perfectly still with her eyes squeezed shut that he surely never knew that the heat from his body made her reel with the possibilities of the situation. If she had brushed against him just once, she might have exploded into a thousand little pieces of fire.

Let him think she was made of ice. Let him think she slept when he couldn't. Let him think she was impervious to wind and rain and fear and passion. It was better than the truth, better than admitting she was afraid of getting involved with someone whose eyes could look so deeply into hers, that she was afraid he would see all the things she kept hidden behind her facade of fearless leader.

With this facade carefully back in place, she turned to see him staring out the window. He looked around and gave her an infectious grin that made her smile back. She forced herself to face front again. It was just the same as any other trip, she told herself; the same excitement, the same thrill of sharing experiences with a new group of people. With just one person, the experience was bound to be different—more intense, more personal. But that didn't mean she should lose control of her emotions before they'd taken the first step on their way to the Manang Valley.

She pressed her hands against her temples and had a stern talk with herself. She gave herself a series of reminders: reminders of who she was and what she wanted out of life; reminders of why she was going on this trip with the very attractive and very dedicated doctor who was sitting behind her—who had the power with one dazzling smile to make her forget all of the above. This was not going to be an easy trip. But she had the feeling it would be one she would always remember.

At Pokhara they met Kibo, the Sherpa, and the three hoisted the gear onto their shoulders. With Kyla in the lead, they were actually at the trailhead by midmorning.

They stopped by a small spring, and while Chase filled their canteens with water Kyla spread the map out on a flat rock and she and Kibo put their elbows on the rock and discussed their route. Chase leaned over her shoulder and she felt his arm brush against the back of her neck. She made a supreme effort not to notice the shivers his touch sent traveling up and down her spine. When she spoke, she kept her eyes on the map.

"We'll be following the Marysandi River." She trailed a steady finger along a blue line on the map. "Then we'll cut back between the Annapurnas on the west and Manaslu and Himalchuli on the east."

"How far can we get today?" Chase's voice was charged with energy and a touch of impatience.

"Probably about this far." She indicated a fraction of an inch and she felt his body stiffen.

"I hope you're not holding back because of me," he told her. "I can keep up."

"I'm sure you can." Kyla turned to look at him and found his face so close to hers she could see flecks of yellow in his deep brown eyes. She wondered what would happen if she leaned toward him and tilted her head up so that her lips brushed his. She drew herself up and rocked back and forth. What was wrong with her? Maybe she ought to listen to her own speeches once in a while—the ones that explained her philosophy of trekking, which echoed her philosophy of life.

Now was the time to establish her authority. She was the leader, he was the follower. He wasn't going to like it, but that was the way it was.

"We take it easy the first day, to get used to the climate, the change of altitude." She paused and looked down at her feet.

"We're almost into November," he protested. "If the snow comes early and blocks the passes—"

"Chase," she interrupted, "I know about the snow and the passes. I've been here before, remember? That's why I'm taking you." She put her hand on his shoulder, then instantly regretted it. "Everyone's eager to get going the first day,'' she said, knowing that Chase Cunningham was not everyone.

If she'd felt this undercurrent flowing between herself and anyone else, she would have quit right away, baled out while she still had her wits about her. Why wasn't she doing it now? She removed her hand from his shoulder and he studied her face, waiting for her to continue.

''But you have to pace yourself,'' she added. The skeptical look in his eyes disturbed her. She took a deep breath and quoted from the Adventure Travel catalog:

'' 'The morning walk and the afternoon walk each lasts about three to four hours with a break of two hours at a scenic point during which a hot lunch is prepared.' ''

She thought she saw a flicker of warmth in his eyes and she rushed on, hoping he'd decided to be reasonable. '' 'Campsites are chosen for their scenic appeal—' ''

''Could we skip the scenic appeal and the two-hour hot lunches?'' he asked. ''We're on a mission, not a vacation. No wonder we have a deforestation problem here, what with trekkers eating hot lunches every day.''

Kyla glared at him and persisted. '' 'And their proximity to water.' '' She folded the map and stuffed it into her back pocket. ''Sure, we can ignore the highest and most beautiful mountains in the world. We can skip the hot lunches, too, although Kibo here will be cooking on a small propane stove. But that's shortsighted. The trip takes twenty-four days no matter how you do it, unless you're a Sherpa and you use these trails every day.''

She looked over her shoulder at Kibo, whose legs were well muscled. ''These trips are not for restless travelers, the ones who are checking off cathedrals as they go. They're for people who want to see millet being ground with a foot hammer and men twisting dry grass into skeins. I can't force you to look up at the mountains or eat Kibo's hot potato *rosti*, but after all those months staring at the green walls of the operating room, I would think—''

Chase swung his day pack onto his shoulders and kicked the heel of his boot in the dirt. ''You would think I'd want to take time out to smell the daisies, wouldn't you? Well, people have been telling me that all my life, but I've got other plans. Did you ever think about all the people in the world who can't see the mountains because they can't see, who can't smell the daisies because they can't see to get where the flowers are? I think about them all the time, and I don't want to waste any more time talking about it. We'll do it your way because you're the guide, and we'll continue our philosophical discussion at the campsite with its proximity to water.'' With that pointed remark, he turned and set off down the trail.

Kyla glanced briefly at Kibo, who nodded and ran on ahead of Chase to take the lead. Her throat was tight with anger. The implication was clear. She was trying to turn a humanitarian voyage into a joyride. He was humane and caring; she was superficial, out for a good time. Damn him and his holier-than-thou attitude. Let him walk all day without food or water if he wanted.

She would stop for lunch, she would listen to the reedy flute music of the mountains and she would admire the most spectacular peaks that existed. Her day pack bounced against her back as she strode forward, trying to ignore Chase, who was a good fifty yards in front of her.

Chase stared straight ahead as the trail narrowed, determined not to turn around to see how far Kyla was behind. He knew she'd be swinging along, her lithe body in tune with nature, her curly brown hair framing her face that would be lifted to the sky and watching for the first glimpse of a snow-covered peak.

His mouth was dry and his stomach contracted with hunger. He'd been walking for only two hours and he wished he could take back every word he'd said that morning—especially the part about not wanting a hot lunch.

He wanted a hot lunch and he wanted Kyla Tanner; and it looked as if he wasn't going to get either one—not on this trip, anyway. What was he doing wrong? Coming off sounding like a smug, self-satisfied do-gooder, for one thing, he decided. He stopped in the middle of the trail to reconsider his position.

Groves of pipal and banana trees lined both sides of the path. Pushing his way through the thick foliage, he stood under branches heavy with ripe fruit. Small red bananas almost fell into his hands. He heard footsteps and shoved the branches aside. It had to be Kyla, and he had to apologize. He saw her before she saw him because she wasn't looking straight ahead. She was looking down at her feet and she was limping.

"Kyla."

She glanced up, startled at the sound of his voice.

He plunged through the dense growth and grabbed her by the arm. "What's wrong?"

Her eyes were cool, gray—the color of slate. She hesitated, obviously trying to decide whether to admit there was anything wrong at all.

"I'm breaking in new boots," she finally answered, pulling away from his grasp. "It's always difficult the first day."

"Let me look."

She shook her head. "I have some moleskin to put on when we stop for lunch."

"I hope it's soon," he said. "Haven't you heard that an army marches on its stomach?"

She shook her head in disbelief. He held out his hand. "Want a banana?" he asked.

"Thanks." She turned and led the way this time, peeling her banana as she walked, still with a limp.

He frowned. "Do you always start out with new boots?" He stayed as close to her as he could without stepping on her heels.

"I never do," she replied over her shoulder. "But at the end of the last trip I promised my old boots to the Sherpa. I thought I was going rafting and I'd have time to break in new ones before I went climbing again. And then Lillian fell on her back, and you know the rest."

He did. And he also knew she'd rather be on the white waters of some river than here with him—probably almost anywhere but here with him. He wasn't sure why she was on this trip at all, but now her feet hurt and it was his fault.

He swallowed his pride. "When do we stop? I want to look at your feet."

"No, you don't. You want to eat lunch."

"That, too," he admitted. "If I said I was wrong, would you stop?"

"Right or wrong, we're stopping at a clearing up ahead. Kibo probably has the stove going already." She paused and he almost bumped into her. "But I warn you, it's a scenic spot." Her mouth turned up at the corners.

He felt a sense of relief. Maybe she wasn't angry anymore. "I can handle it," he assured her. "Or if it's too scenic, I can close my eyes."

She nodded agreeably and they walked in silence for the next fifteen minutes while the vegetation changed from lush jungle to flat rice fields. He smelled the potatoes cooking before he saw the clearing at the edge of the river. Kibo was bent over the stove turning a potato pancake stuffed with onions, carrots, celery and cabbage. On the other side of the stream, women stood patiently in the furrows of the fields, fishing.

Chase dropped his pack and sat down on a large blanket that Kibo had spread out. Kyla settled down across from him and he reached for the laces of her boot.

She drew her knees up against her chest. "I can do it."

He moved closer and pulled one boot toward him. "Let me." She pressed her lips together tightly and he wondered how long she'd been walking in pain. He tugged gently at her sock and Kyla gasped involuntarily when it brushed against an ugly red blister. He held the arch of her foot, his fingers cool against her skin. She closed her eyes and tilted her head back.

"I wish we had caught it before it burst," he said mildly. "If you hadn't been so stubborn..."

"I'm stubborn? You were in a hurry," she reminded him.

"Not that much of a hurry." He reached for his pack and pulled out some gauze and antibiotic cream. She sighed and rested her head against her pack and let him apply the cream and then tape the gauze over the gaping broken blister. He placed her foot on his thigh and looked at her thoughtfully.

"My God, you must think I'm a monster if you thought I wouldn't stop for you." He ran his fingers over the ball of her foot, lightly massaging her toes.

She shrugged and closed her eyes, letting the pleasurable sensations wash over her. No one had ever told her the foot was an erogenous zone. "It doesn't matter," she heard herself mutter.

"It matters to me." He was unlacing the other boot now and pulling her sock off. Then he had both her feet in his hands and was doing incredible things with those skillful fingers she'd watched so often, wondering how they'd feel on her. Now she knew. They felt... as if they could mold her into any shape he wanted. Her whole body was on fire. How would it be if his hands kept moving up her, doing whatever he wanted, whatever she wanted.

She felt the friction of his fingers against her skin and sensations pulsated wildly inside her. She was losing control. "Chase," she said, "I'm all right now. I'm fine. Thank you." She opened her eyes and sat up. He let her go, watching her with a half smile, his eyes dark and soft as brown velvet.

Kibo stood over them, offering each of them a steaming plate of potato *rosti*, and they ate without speaking. She was afraid Chase knew the effect he'd had on her. She would have to be more careful not to let that happen again. It would be better for her if he continued to be obnoxious as he'd been this morning, rather than kind and attentive. It would be too easy to like him too much if he showed this side of himself often.

He put his fork down, and as if he'd read her thoughts, he said, "I was obnoxious this morning. I'm sorry."

"Don't apologize," she replied brusquely. "You were right. This isn't a vacation. We're on a mission. I'll try to remember that."

"No, you were right." He leaned back on his elbows and watched the women in the fields with their straw hats and bright skirts. "Sometimes I wish I could stand knee-deep in a stream and hold a fishing line all day just like that, but there's so much to do and so little time."

She nodded and took a cup of tea from Kibo. "I know, I feel the same way. Only I'm doing something else with my time, usually something pretty selfish." He shook his head, but she continued. "You're wrapped up in your work, in helping others. I'm wrapped up in myself, in filling my life with challenges. Sometimes you make me feel pretty shabby."

He put his hand on her knee. "If you were wrapped up in yourself you wouldn't be here right now. You'd be off on your raft trip. You would never have stayed with Lillian. And what about helping me in the operating room? You're right about one thing though. You do fill your life with challenges."

Kyla gave him a long look, then she emptied her cup on the ground. She carefully placed the moleskin over the gauze, tied up her boots and stood.

Chase looked up at her as if he were trying to make up his mind about something. Had she told him too much? Or not enough? She held out her hand and he reached for it and let her pull him up until he stood so close to her the tips of their boots touched. Then his hands were on her arms and his face so close to hers she held her breath.

She wanted him to kiss her—just once—to get it over with. Then she'd know how his lips felt and she could stop imagining it. But when he did, it was just a token, just a brush of his mouth across hers. He dropped his hands and picked up his pack as if nothing had happened.

She was left standing there feeling cheated and let down—and angry with herself for feeling that way. If he had kissed her the way she wanted to be on this first day, where would they be on day twenty-four? Images raced through her mind as they trudged along the trail again. She was glad Chase was behind her so she couldn't see his broad shoulders, his easy gait, his dark hair almost touching the collar of his damp cotton shirt. Everything would be all right once they got out of this muggy, sensuous valley, she thought. In the crisp mountain air she would not let Chase touch her or her emotions. Then she wouldn't feel the way she did now: nervous, vulnerable, exposed.

The afternoon sun shone relentlessly as Chase and Kyla climbed past forests of bamboo. The warm, humid air coated Kyla's skin with a film of perspiration, and her feet felt as heavy as the stones that lined the path. Hill tribes passed them on their way down to the village below, and Kyla smiled at the women dressed in rich burgundy jackets that were decorated with strands of yellow and orange beads.

She and Chase stepped off the trail to let the natives glide past in their long, wrap skirts, and Kyla saw them look Chase steadily in the eye, their gazes full of pride, curiosity and frank admiration.

For a moment she saw him through their eyes. A tall man in wrinkled khaki pants, with a wide, generous mouth and dark eyes that stared back, returning their curiosity. Did he return their admiration, too? Suddenly Kyla felt plain and ordinary compared to those exotic creatures now out of sight.

It was still warm at dusk when they stopped for the night by the side of the muddy Kondori River, frothing from the fall glacial runoff. If Chase was impressed by the wild flow, he didn't say anything. He just stood watching Kibo haul in fish for their dinner. When he turned and saw Kyla standing behind him, he frowned.

"Get off your feet," he ordered.

She nodded and went to the campsite to take off her boots. The blister throbbed insistently, and she watched gratefully while Kibo made dahl with rice and set up a makeshift table under the branches.

They ate without speaking; the rumble of the river against rocks took the place of conversation and background music. The fish was crisp and delicious, and afterward Kibo served *raksi* in small glasses. The potent local drink eased the pain in Kyla's foot and she almost forgot about her argument with Chase that morning.

She leaned against a sun-heated rock and felt it warm her back. Chase sat across the clearing on an old tree stump, holding his glass and looking past the river.

"You were right," he said.

"About what?"

"The scenic campsite and smelling the daisies."

She smiled to herself. Maybe it would work out after all. Maybe this trek wasn't so different from the others, with the usual first-day jitters, the usual argument with the trekker who challenged the leader. Who was she kidding? There had never been anyone like Chase on any of her tours. There had never been anyone like him anywhere—not in her entire life.

The river gurgled and splashed in the distance. Kibo had inflated the mattresses and laid the sleeping bags out, and then melted away in the darkness to get his rest. Kyla couldn't see Chase anymore, but she sensed he was looking at her, and it made her uneasy.

She absentmindedly rubbed the sole of her foot. The silence was uncomfortable. Was it because she owed him an apology? Was that what he was waiting for? She cleared her throat.

"I don't have the right to tell you how to live your life. We'll smell the daisies along the trail, but I do realize that most doctors are too busy to take much time off for their real lives."

"My father isn't." Chase's voice came out of the dusk. "He takes every Wednesday off to play golf. He thinks I'm crazy to work this hard for almost nothing. So does my mother. So did my fiancée—ex-fiancée."

"Is that the reason she's your ex-fiancée?" Kyla never asked personal questions of her group. That way, they wouldn't ask them of her, and she could keep her secrets to herself. But here, by the side of a rushing river, in the balmy night air, a million miles from nowhere, she tilted her head back and looked at the stars and thought of all the things she wanted to know about Chase Cunningham.

"That she thought I was crazy? No, not the only reason." His voice seemed detached, with just a hint of bitterness. "She didn't want to come to Nepal, and she didn't want to live on a shoestring. She wanted to stay in Piedmont where I could make a decent living."

"Was that so bad?"

"Do you know what the doctor/patient ratio is in California?"

"One to twenty?"

"You're close. And do you know how many people go without medical care in Nepal? Of course you do. You've been to the villages. My God, if I could get my father over here..."

"Why can't you?"

"It's too late. He has a practice and a wife and a house and an expensive life-style to support. All the things I don't want."

"Including the wife?" The words escaped her.

Kyla could hear Chase stand and begin pacing around. "If it hadn't been for my mother, my father could have done something like this, instead of tummy tucks and liposections and face-lifts on vain women."

The air was still and warm, but every time Chase said "wife" or "woman" Kyla felt a cold chill. "I thought that's what plastic surgeons did."

"There are all kinds of plastic surgeons."

Kyla shifted her position, but she kept her eyes on the stars and her voice steady. "There are all kinds of women, too. They're not all vain or looking for a meal ticket."

"Of course not." He sounded surprised. "Did I say that?"

"You said you didn't want a wife." She tried to sound casual, almost uninterested.

Chase stopped pacing and stared into the darkness, wishing he could see her face. Her slightly husky voice enchanted him and he wanted her to keep talking, but hearing her voice wasn't enough. He wanted to see if there was a gleam in her eyes or whether her mouth was tilted up or turned down.

"I didn't," he answered, and then he wondered if it was still true. "Actually the problem isn't that I don't want a wife. The problem is that wives don't want me. I can't blame them. I'm hard to get along with. I want my own way, and the nicest thing I own is half of a Tibetan carpet I'm storing in my apartment. So you can see why no one wants me."

"I told you that carpet is all yours," she insisted.

"Do you think that would help?"

"Help you find a wife who wants to marry a doctor who takes his pay in yak butter and bananas and orders her around, besides? I doubt it." She smiled to herself. With or without money or a gentle bedside manner, Chase had to be the best catch that had ever escaped from Piedmont, California, or anywhere this side of the Himalayas. But she'd die before she'd ever admit it.

"What about you?" His voice was closer now. She heard his footsteps and saw his shape approaching. "Doesn't anyone want you, either?" he asked softly.

"That's right," she answered smoothly, grateful to him for providing the out. "Tour guides make rotten wives. We love to give orders, too. And we're addicted to excitement...."

Chase was standing in front of her now. Her words trailed off when he reached down and pulled her up to face him. She was going to tell him how her knees knocked and her heart pounded every time she saw Mount Everest at sunrise, but her knees were knocking right now and the only thing she could see was Chase. The smell of his skin made her heart pound.

His hands slid up her arms and he framed her face with his fingers. "We have a lot in common," he said. His lips touched hers—lightly at first. Then, when he felt her arms go around him and her body melt into his, he covered her mouth with his. He tasted the sweetness of the rice wine and the sweetness of Kyla until they blended. He forgot that she was only his guide, and that this was only the first day of a very long trip. It wasn't hard to get addicted to excitement. And Kyla Tanner was the most exciting woman he had ever met.

Chapter Six

Chase wasn't surprised when Kyla abruptly pulled away and announced it was bedtime. He was getting used to her quick changes in mood. He didn't understand them, but he was determined to find out what made her melt into his arms one moment and then the next, turn into a camp counselor.

He stood watching her pour water from the canteen into a cup with a steady hand. He was still breathing hard and his body ached to hold her again, but he was afraid it was a feeling she didn't share.

"You'll have to forgive me for that," he said. "This is my first trek, and I didn't know the procedure. Are you going to play taps and then have a bed check next?"

She turned and looked at him. By the pale light of the sliver of a moon, he could see her mouth tighten. "Chase, we've talked about this over and over. I've told you how I feel about relationships with men in my group. Naturally there are bound to be attractions on these trips. We're off in the mountains alone. There are mutual needs. Men fall for the leader, the leader falls for the men. It happens all the time, but—"

"It gets tiresome," he interrupted. "I understand completely. Another trek, another man falling for the leader. I can see why you've set up your rules. Along with all of my other faults, I'm slow at catching on. You see, this is a special trip for me, and you're a special person. At least I think you are, but I'll never know unless you give me a chance to find out. Don't shut me out, Kyla."

She shook her head and he thought her eyes glistened with unshed tears, but she turned her back to him so fast he couldn't be sure. When she spoke, her voice was muffled.

"You were the one who reminded me that we're on a medical mission and not a vacation. This isn't the Bahamas, after all. When I told you to take time out to look at the scenery, I didn't mean . . ." She hesitated.

"You didn't mean to take advantage of you after you'd had two glasses of *raksi* after dinner. All right, I get the message. But are you telling me you didn't feel anything when I kissed you?" Frustrated, he wanted to grab her and turn her around so she would have to deny it to his face, but her shoulders slumped and she didn't speak.

He walked away, slowing hoping that the answer was no. She must have felt something, too. Maybe she didn't know what it was, but she couldn't deny that it was there and that it was real. Because that was how he felt.

He unzipped his sleeping bag and laid it on top of the inflated mattress. Then he stretched out on his back. When he heard her walk toward him and heard the scrape of her shirt and shorts against her sleeping bag, he covered his eyes with his arm and finally fell asleep.

* * *

It wasn't morning when he woke up, but Kyla was bending over him, so close and smelling so fresh that he thought it must be a dream.

"Chase, wake up."

He sat up so quickly he bumped her chin with his head. When she put her cool hand against his forehead, he knew he must be dreaming.

"I'm sorry," she said softly, "but Kibo says there's a woman in labor in the village up the river. Will you come?"

He nodded and reached for his shoes. "What's the problem?"

"They say she's in terrible pain, that it's lasted too long."

He stood and frowned. "Too long? How long?"

Kyla rubbed her palms against her shorts. "I don't know. I know what you're going to say. Labor *is* painful and it does go on for a long time, but I know these people. They're tough and they don't complain unless it's really serious. Maybe it's just a normal delivery, but Kibo thought, and I thought..." She met Chase's gaze and bit her lip.

"I'll get a few things," he replied, and Kyla breathed a sigh of relief. He was so calm and radiated so much reassurance that Kyla knew if she were sick and needed help, there was no one she'd rather have at her side than Chase.

He didn't have a little black bag, but he packed instruments and medicine in his backpack. Then they followed Kibo along the river for a few kilometers until they saw lights from a clearing. Out of the darkness a group of people clustered around them and Kyla felt the tension in the air. A man hurried forward and spoke to Kibo in a low voice.

"He says the baby is coming now. Will you come please?"

They followed the two men around the back of a low brick building where Chase stopped to wash his hands under an outdoor spigot. When he finished he nodded to Kyla.

"You scrub, too."

"Me?"

"I may need you." He touched her shoulder and gave her a reassuring smile. "I know I'll need you," he said firmly.

The native gestured them on to a small hut and pulled back the curtain at the entrance. Together they walked inside. In the center of the room, illuminated by the dim light from a kerosene lantern, Kyla saw a woman tossing and turning on a thin cot, her body swollen. A smaller, older woman in a long shapeless garment stood by, watching and wringing her hands. Without hesitating, Kyla asked her to bring clean cloths and hot water.

Then she sat on the edge of the bed and timed the contractions while Chase measured to see how far the woman's cervix was dilated. Her large eyes filling with tears, the woman in labor moaned and pointed to her back.

Chase frowned. "Back pains," he explained, and Kyla gently rolled the woman onto her side and began massaging her. As the contractions increased in intensity, Kyla braced herself against the floor and kneaded deeply to ease the pressure. Perspiration pouring from her face, the woman shuddered in pain and Chase listened for a fetal heartbeat with his stethoscope.

Hours passed and at last the contractions were coming every two minutes. Kyla's hands were numb, the muscles in her arms ached. But she mopped the woman's brow and whispered words of encouragement in English and Nepali.

When Chase finally delivered the baby—it was a boy—he had to hold it upside down by the feet and slap it to start it breathing. Kyla thought that was the longest moment of her life. The cries that filled the small room brought tears to her eyes, and when Chase cut the cord and placed the baby in the woman's arms, she had to turn away for fear she would collapse with relief and happiness.

She caught Chase's eye for a moment and tried to hide her tears. For him it must just have been another delivery. But for her it was a miracle. With one last look at the baby in his mother's arms, Kyla tiptoed out of the room and Chase followed her.

They walked slowly back along the river to their campsite. "First time you've seen a delivery?" Chase asked over his shoulder.

"Yes," she answered breathlessly, still shaken by the experience.

"Now you'll know what to expect when you're on the other side."

Kyla swallowed hard. "What?"

"You'll be prepared for your own baby's birth. You'll know what to expect." He continued his steady pace over rocks and around bushes.

Kyla squinted up at the pale blue morning sky. "I don't think so. I'm not planning to have any children. I'm not even going to get married." She watched his pack sway against his broad back, and thought about the power he had to save lives. He slowed down and Kyla jerked to a stop.

"Why not?"

"Why not?" she repeated. Fortunately he resumed his brisk pace and she tried to speak in a normal voice. "I thought it was obvious. What would I do with a husband? I'm always gone, I'd never be at home. What kind of a marriage would that be?"

He didn't answer and Kyla didn't know whether he couldn't hear her over the roar of the rushing river or he didn't know what to say. She felt an overwhelming urge to explain, but she couldn't say that no one who suspected she might be carrying the gene for Huntington's disease would be stupid or careless enough to get married and bring children into the world. She desperately needed to maintain her usual smoke screen. And even more desperately, she needed Chase to believe her.

"As for children," she continued, "what would I do with them? Can you see me with a baby in my backpack?" She was watching the trail, her eyes on the roots and rocks, when Chase suddenly turned. Before she knew it, she had run into his arms.

"Yes," he said, looking at her as if he'd never seen her before. "I can see you with a baby in your backpack, a baby with gray eyes and a hat to keep the sun off her face."

Chase's hands were on her shoulders and she pressed her lips together to keep from crying. "Her?" she murmured. It was one thing to talk about a hypothetical baby, but to give it gray eyes and a hat was going too far.

She raised her hands to grip his arms and they stood locked together. "I don't want a husband or a baby. They don't fit into my plans. I thought you knew." Kyla heard her voice rise. Chase shook his head. What did she have to do to make him understand? She took a deep breath.

"Maybe it isn't apparent to you, but my life is perfect the way it is. I have nobody waiting for me to come home, nobody nagging me to stop taking chances—nobody, nobody." The look in Chase's eyes had deepened, darkened, until instead of the envy she expected to see, there was something close to pity, the one thing she couldn't accept.

Her tears started to fall uncontrollably and Chase pulled her to him. She sobbed against his chest. "Dammit," she protested, her voice shaking, "why don't you believe me?"

He ran his fingers through her hair and held her until her body stopped trembling. Knowing his shirt was soaked with her tears, she pulled back but the tears kept coming. She didn't want his pity, but she did want his arms around her. She had never felt so confused.

"I do believe you," he assured her, drying her face with his fingertips, then offering her his handkerchief.

She blew her nose. "Good. Thank you. I don't know why I let loose like that. It had nothing to do with you." She managed a small smile to cover her lie. It had everything to do with him.

He took her hand and guided her along the path. "It's been a long night," he explained. "And we brought a baby into the world. It was an emotional experience. You're allowed to cry."

She kept her hand in his and followed him through the trees. "I may be allowed to cry, but I can't take credit for the baby. You did that. What are you, anyway? I thought you were an eye doctor, but I saw you deliver a baby and now you're telling me when to cry. Are you a psychiatrist, too?"

He laughed and pulled her toward him, and side by side they walked into their campsite. The sound of his merriment and his arm around her shoulders sent a wave of warmth through her body.

Kibo was waiting for them with hot tea, and Chase motioned Kyla to sit next to him on a flat rock. The first rays of the sun lighted the banks of the river ahead of them.

"Are you too young to know what a G.P. is?" Chase asked in answer to her question. "That's what I am, only we call them family practitioners now."

She looked at him. "You can do everything," she said, and she believed it.

He shook his head and the sun picked up glints in his hair. "Not everything."

She couldn't look away from him. A sense of peace came over her, a feeling of well-being. It was a new day, and she was a new woman, purged by the tears she'd shed and renewed by the miracle of birth; and touched by this man who sat next to her, who radiated warmth and compassion and something else. What was it? She turned her head. She was reading too much into his actions. He was a doctor, trained to take care of the sick and needy; a man with a strong sense of duty.

Chase drank his tea, glad to have something to do but stare at Kyla. Her cheeks were flushed, her eyes still glistened with tears. He couldn't stop thinking of her in that makeshift delivery room. She had massaged the woman's back, kept a cool cloth on her forehead and timed her contractions as if she'd been doing it all her life. Instead, she'd been climbing and camping and shooting rapids.

She seemed to be afraid of only one thing—him. What had he done to deserve that? Was it his talking about a baby? She claimed she didn't want anyone to share her life, but he saw the longing that she tried to hide. He could picture her so clearly with an infant that he could see himself reaching out and touching it and feeling the little fingers wrap around his hand.

Chase abruptly set down his cup and began repacking his knapsack. What on earth was he thinking about? He ordered himself to imagine working eighteen hours a day and having a family, too. He could assume how demanding a wife could be. She would be a drain on your time, a drain on your finances and a drain on your emotions. He of all people should understand why Kyla didn't want to get married. There was nothing like being free, unencumbered, in charge of your life, was there?

But there was another feeling creeping up on him, one he couldn't shake. It was the feeling he got when Kyla looked at him under wet lashes, or when he touched her or kissed her. It was tenderness, it was excitement. And it was something else. He zipped his bag closed.

"Maybe we should take the day off," he suggested. "You didn't get much sleep last night."

She shook her head and stood. "I feel fine. I feel great, in fact. And we don't have any time to lose." She looked up at the bluffs, and Chase followed her gaze. There were no snow-capped peaks in sight, but they were there, somewhere over the next rise, or around the next hill, and until they saw them, they were still far from their goal.

"Good girl." There was a new look on her face that Chase had never seen before. The lines around her mouth were relaxed, her eyes were as clear as the morning sky. He wanted to touch her hair again, lift it off the back of her neck and kiss her. But if he did, he wouldn't want to stop, and he might forget why they were here and where they were going.

Kyla wouldn't, though. He smiled wryly to himself. And she'd probably pull back the way she had the last time. What was it that made her so tough and so strong and independent one minute and a puddle of tears the next? Why was she here, anyway? When she'd suggested taking him he was too stunned to look for a motive—too stunned and too grateful and too excited.

He'd find out, he promised himself. If it took twenty-four days, he would find out why and how and who she really was.

They were on the trail half an hour later. Corn had replaced rice in the fields, and a waterfall came down from somewhere far above them. Kyla led them off the trail down a path behind the fall. The spray dampened their shorts and shirts, and Kyla stuck her head out to let the water run through her hair. Chase ached to hold her hair in his hands and run his fingers through it.

She shook her head and showered him with drops of water. "It's cold," she said.

Kibo had miraculously come up with a towel from deep in the duffel bag. Chase intercepted it and wrapped it around her hair and massaged gently. He pulled her toward him, away from the waterfall, with his hands on her temples. Chase saw Kibo glide away out of sight. The man had an uncanny sense of when to disappear.

With the towel twisted on top of her head, she looked like a nymph he had just found living under the waterfall. She mystified him, she bewitched him, she was driving him crazy. Her lips parted and met his. He sighed, a ragged sound coming from deep in his throat. Instead of pulling back, she lifted her arms and held him tightly as if she had been wanting this to happen as much as he did. The kiss deepened, lengthened. The sound of the water, the mist rising in the air and the taste of her, filled him with unbearable pleasure.

He finally held her at arm's length and looked at her. What were all those pressing questions he wanted to ask her? He drew his eyebrows together.

"Why?" he began.

She shrugged and smiled. "Who knows why?"

He unwrapped the towel and her hair fell loose. "I didn't mean why did you kiss me. I meant why did you offer to come along in the first place, and yes, why did you kiss me?" He gave her a lopsided grin, but she turned and Chase was left staring at the back of her head.

"Impulse," she explained lightly. "Sometimes I operate that way. You needed a guide, I decided to be your guide. I cried because I saw a new life come into the world this morning. It's old hat for you, but for me it was something special. As for the kiss—" she held out her hands, palms up, and kept walking "—what can I say? It was the mist and the morning and the moment . . . and it was wrong, because now you're trying to read something into it that wasn't there."

Chase grabbed her arm and turned her toward him. "Look at me when you say that. Because it meant a lot more to me than the mist and the morning. There was something there. I felt it and you felt it, too. And I have another question. Why are you so afraid to admit it? Impulse? I don't believe you." He let her arm fall and stomped ahead of her.

How much longer was she going to play this game? He felt her anger as they hiked in silence, following the equally silent Kibo down the gorge. Cornfields gave way to dense mixed forests and occasional stands of pine trees. A brisk wind started blowing. Chase reached for a sweater from his pack, then turned to look at Kyla, ten yards behind him, still in short sleeves, her hair hanging in wet strands.

He waited until she caught up with him. Her glance flickered over him, then she carefully stepped around him. He didn't care how angry she was, he wasn't going to let her get sick.

"Put on your sweater."

"I'm not cold."

"Your hair's still wet." He blocked the trail so she couldn't get around him. "Kibo," he called as if he were in surgery, "the towel."

She clenched her teeth while he rubbed her hair briskly. There was nothing sensual in his touch this time, nothing for her to complain about. He was a doctor; the patient was wet and cold. He looked at her critically. Her hair made a damp halo around her face, but her expression was not angelic.

"Are you finished?" she asked.

"The sweater," he requested patiently.

"It's in my pack." She turned stiffly, and he slipped the pack off of her back. Her shoulders were rigid. When he found her sweater he pulled it over her head and he nodded.

"That's better."

"Since when did you get to be my guardian?" she demanded. "I've been climbing mountains for years and no one's ever told me when to put my sweater on or dried my hair for me."

"Not even your mother?" he asked calmly.

Her voice softened. "My mother didn't climb mountains. Most of the time I was growing up she wasn't well. My father took me and he had the sense to leave me alone—more sense than you have."

The words stung as she had intended them to, but Chase stood watching her, waiting for her to stop. "There's been a change in the weather," he said. "Even experienced hikers can get carried away with the scenery and forget to take care of themselves. If you get hypothermia we'll be set back a day or two and we can't afford the time." He ran his hand down her arm as if to test her body heat, but she shook him off.

"Let's go," she announced.

This time she took the lead and they didn't stop until lunch in a pine grove high above the clear stream that thrashed below. Kibo had concocted a savory soup and they ate in awkward silence.

"What happened to your mother?" he inquired finally.

She looked at him over her cup of soup. "She got progressively worse and she died when I was twenty."

"How long had she been sick?"

She sighed as if he had used up all her patience. "A long time. Ever since I can remember." She set her cup down and studied the toes of her boots. "Could we talk about something else? It's hard for me, even now. . . ."

"I'm sorry. Sometimes it helps to talk about it."

"Well, this time it doesn't." She stood. "Are you ready?"

"Sure."

He was so sure of himself. Kyla wanted to force him to wear his sweater and pry into his private life. The worst part was that he was right. She had been cold, but she didn't want to take the time to put on her sweater or dry her hair. Even if tortured, she would never admit he'd been right.

He had tortured her, there by the waterfall. His kiss was the most exquisite torture she could ever imagine. And she could never let it happen again. It wasn't his fault he had the wrong idea about her. She had let it happen, she had wanted it to happen, maybe she had even made it happen. She shivered at the memory of his warm lips on hers.

He was watching her. "What's wrong?"

She felt a flush creep up her neck. "Nothing. Thanks to you, I'm warm and dry and I'm ready to go." She gave him a tentative smile, and he smiled back, a slow lazy smile that melted all her remaining resentment. He held out his hand.

"Friends?"

"Friends." She breathed a sigh of relief. They were back to where they had started—before the kiss, the hurt, the emotion of the morning.

With a light step Kyla followed Chase to the trail. Overhead, coal-black ravens circled in the cloudless sky. By late afternoon they had walked through a small settlement, had been stared at by toothless old women and had passed by packs of donkeys wearing bells.

"This used to be a major path between Nepal and Tibet," Kyla explained. "Until they put in the suspension bridge." She looked down through the pine trees to the river below. "It's made a big difference." Around the curve the narrow footbridge came into view, a long ribbon of steel, suspended above a tributary of the Paundi Khola river.

"Do we have to use the bridge?" Chase's voice was casual.

Kyla slowed her steps. "If we want to get to the other side."

"I mean, people got to the other side before they built the bridge, so why don't we use the other way, whatever it was?" Chase suggested.

Kyla stopped. "Crossing the river is a much shorter route. That's why they built this bridge." She turned around. Chase's face was pale. "You're not afraid of heights, are you?"

"Me?" His voice was incredulous. "Would I suggest a trip to the mountains if I had acrophobia? I'm only afraid of bridges."

"Don't look down," she said.

"That's easy for you to say."

"I'll hold your hand," she offered. Not many men would admit to being afraid of anything, she thought. He appeared to be glued to the spot he was standing on.

"Both hands?" he asked with a tight smile.

She smiled back encouragingly.

"Oh, God."

"Chase." She took his hands in hers and pulled him toward her. Her eyes held his gaze, telling him he wouldn't fall, that she would not let him fall. She walked slowly backward onto the bridge, looking over her shoulder, pulling him with her. The bridge swayed in the wind. He gripped her hands so tightly she thought they might be attached for life.

"Don't look now," she cautioned, "but there's a little village down there. It's called Palenksangu, because once a long time ago there was a plank bridge here. Plank came to be Palenk and *sangu* is the Nepali word for bridge." His eyes were locked with hers, but she didn't think he heard anything she said. You must listen to me, Chase, she silently prayed; and don't look down, just keep listening.

"That's fascinating," Chase said between clenched teeth. "Got any more stories?"

"The goddess Lakshmi is coming soon. I've never been in Nepal for the Festival of Lights before, have you?" Think about something else, anything but the bridge and the long drop to the river below. Please, Chase.

He shook his head. "At this rate I don't think I'll be around for it this year, either." His face glistened with sweat.

"Yes, you will, and she'll come through your window or your door and inspect your account books. And if she's pleased with what she sees, she'll bestow prosperity on you for the next year." Just a few more steps. Come on, you can do it.

"I'm not interested in prosperity right now. I just want to live long enough to make it across this bridge."

"You can do it," she promised. Her heels left the metal surface and hit dirt. She pulled him off the bridge and hugged him tightly. "See, you did it."

"No, you did it," he replied, with the color back in his face, his mouth relaxed, his voice deep and steady. "Thanks." He bent over and kissed her on the cheek.

That was not what she wanted. They had crossed a bridge together, holding hands so tightly she'd felt a part of him. The adrenaline was still pumping through her body and all he did was to kiss her on the cheek. She felt let down again.

Her mind told her the adventure was over for the day, but her body needed more.

Kibo had made lemonade from powder in an envelope and they sat in the middle of a grove of pines and drank it. She watched Chase finish his drink, then lie down on his back on a carpet of pine needles. "I've got a story for you now," he said.

She nodded, unwilling to speak, afraid her voice would betray her disappointment.

"Once upon a time in the distant land of California, there lived a boy whose parents wanted to get rid of him for the summer."

"Why?"

"So they could go to Europe where his father was attending a medical conference."

Kyla sat up straight trying to see his face, but Chase held his hand over his forehead to shade his eyes from the sunlight.

"So they dropped him off at a camp. It wasn't a survival camp or anything like that. It was just a camp with crafts and volleyball and horseback riding. It was on the Eel River and it was very expensive."

"Did the boy like it?" Kyla turned over to lie on her stomach and inhale the scent of the pine needles.

"I guess he liked it all right. He might have been lonely at first, but that was better than being bored in Europe."

"Would he have been bored in Europe?"

"His parents said he would. Anyway there was a hike one day when the kids went to camp out on the other side of the river with their backpacks and tents. He got to be the leader and lead the kids across the bridge."

He paused and Kyla could no longer hear the roar of the river below or the wind through the trees. The only sound was the beating of her own heart.

"What kind of bridge?"

"A footbridge made of steel rope with planks bolted to it and cable handrails. It looked strong enough, but when he stepped on it one of the cables snapped, followed by the other one. I guess it hadn't been used much over the winter, and they were the first group to use it that summer."

"What happened?"

"The far end broke loose and he grabbed the handrails and he swung back against the cliff. But instead of banging into the rocks, he hit a tree that cushioned the blow." He shook his head. "This kid actually thought he was going to die."

"Go on," she insisted. "Who saved you?"

"Me? What makes you think it was me?" He grinned at her. "I climbed up the planks and we did a different activity that day—water polo or something."

"Climbed up the planks?" she asked incredulously. "Do you mean you weren't even hurt?"

"I got scratched up, and I lost my down sleeping bag and my new backpack."

"And you never crossed another bridge." She looked at him. Instead of a tall, broad-shouldered man with the shadow of a beard and a cleft in his chin, she saw a small scared boy, and she swallowed hard.

"Not until today. And I wouldn't have crossed that one if you hadn't forced me to." He rolled over onto his side and looked at her face. "What's next, fearless leader?" he asked softly.

It was more than she could take. The gleam in his eyes, the smell of the pines and the sound of his voice combined and snapped the last shred of her control just as surely as the cables on the bridge had snapped under Chase's feet. Only this time it was Kyla who went swinging out over the chasm, taking the biggest risk of her life. Her arms wound around Chase's neck and she pulled his face to hers to lose herself in a kiss.

Being lost in the warmth and depth of his mouth was just as she had imagined it would be and then a hundred times better. He shifted until he was on top of her, and their bodies meshed perfectly.

He groaned softly and kissed her eyelids and the hollow in her throat. Then he put his palms flat in the dirt, lifted his head and looked into her eyes.

"It's been quite a day." This time he would not ask for any explanation; he would not risk hearing that she was acting on impulse. Today, they had crossed a bridge together; maybe more than one.

Chapter Seven

The sun was sinking behind the tall trees when Chase rolled over on his back. The look on his face was somewhere between contentment and ecstasy. He stretched his arms and pulled Kyla to him, resting her head against his shoulder.

"Tell Kibo to pitch the tent over our heads. I'm not taking another step."

Kyla smiled, feeling the rough texture of the beginning of a beard. She imagined the snug feeling of being alone together, and sighed with anticipation. A pinecone thudded softly to the ground a few feet away and jarred her out of her reverie. Was she mad? Had she lost all her faculties?

Did she think for one moment that she could sleep next to Chase again and not make love with him? She had done it once, but that was before she knew him, knew the way his voice sounded when he was scared, the way he looked when she woke him in the middle of the night, the way his hands felt on her. Thank God they'd brought two tents.

She didn't have the strength to resist him anymore, but she had to regain it or turn around and go back. Sex was for people who had a clean bill of health—normal people who could also fall in love, get married, have children. People like her could not take the risk. Her college roommate had gotten pregnant though she'd used birth control, and had paid the price—an abortion. Kyla knew Jenny had never quit regretting the baby that never was. The only real birth control was abstinence, at least for herself.

"You have to take another step," she said, standing and holding her hands out to help him up. "We need a campsite with water, and Kibo has gone ahead to buy us a chicken from the village."

He took her hands and let her pull him up. "Okay." He reached for her, but she ducked under his arm. There was a momentary flicker of surprise in his eyes, a hesitation that made her stomach lurch. He must think she turned off and on to see how he'd respond. If she told him the truth, he wouldn't look at her like that. If she told him the truth, he'd understand. And she wanted him to understand. But he'd also feel sorry for her, and that was unacceptable. Anything was better than pity.

"It's not far, and it's all downhill." She put on her backpack with stiff fingers and fumbled with the clasp around her waist. Chase took it out of her hands and fastened it while she watched helplessly.

"Hey," he said, tilting her chin and forcing her to look him in the eye. "If you're worried about what happened back there, don't. It didn't mean any more to me than it did to you. I've finally got it. You're impulsive. You do things and you want to forget about them afterward and not take the consequences, right?"

She tried to protest, but her throat was too tight to speak. She didn't have to explain anything. He'd done it for her.

He thought she was an impulsive idiot who went around throwing herself at men, then pulling back when they got too close. That was okay, wasn't it? No, it wasn't, she reflected as she trudged slowly down the path, but it was better than pity, which was the only alternative.

When they finally reached the clearing at the bottom of the trail Kyla was out of breath and her legs felt like rubber. Where was her stamina? Trekking with Chase was exhausting. In just one day she'd hit the highs and lows, not only physically but emotionally. She stood leaning against a tree, noting the cool, damp air. After a few minutes of rest, she and Chase pitched the tents. Then he wandered off.

Kibo finally appeared, coughing hoarsely and empty-handed. He shook his head and apologized.

"It is the Festival of Moh Puja," he explained. "I had forgotten. The store is closed. But when I explained about the doctor and the memsahib, the owner of the dry-goods shop invited you to the festival tonight."

Kyla closed her eyes. All she wanted to do was to eat Kibo's chicken stew and curl up in her own sleeping bag in her own tent. She didn't want to face any strangers; she especially didn't want to face Chase, and she was sure he felt the same way about her.

As she opened her mouth to make up an excuse, she heard Chase's footsteps behind her. He was not dragging his feet or rubbing his legs. Even in the rapidly descending dusk, she could see the spring in his step and sense the energy in his body.

"A festival?" he asked, looking from Kibo to Kyla. "I've always wanted to know what goes on at those. They don't usually invite strangers. I feel honored, don't you?" He searched Kyla's face and saw fatigue in the lines around her mouth, and stubborn determination in the set of her chin.

"I feel honored," she agreed. "But I also feel tired."

He saw her look longingly at her tent. "You can't be that tired. This is just a normal day's work for you. I'm the one who should be tired. And you're the one who should be urging me to participate in these local rituals."

He ignored the cramps in his legs from the long downhill walk. And he tried to ignore the disappointment he felt when he thought about her off-and-on-again reactions. "Instead of ten people to think about, you only have me. And I only have you," he muttered under his breath. It was better to go to the village—anywhere but here where they'd have to face each other over a bowl of rice and ignore the tension between them.

She shrugged. "Fine. But I hate to tell you that you've already missed the day to worship the crow, the dog and the sacred cow. And also that out of every 365 days, more than 120 are festivals. But—"

"What is Moh Puja?" he interrupted.

"The day to worship oneself. That's appropriate."

"For who?" he asked. "You or me?"

"Me, of course. You're a dedicated doctor, doing things for others."

He gave her a long look. "I haven't noticed you worshiping yourself."

"Haven't you? Well, I don't have to when I have a group around me who do what I tell them to and don't give me any flak." Her voice was light but it was too dark to see the expression on her face.

Kibo lit a lantern and coughed again. Chase frowned and said he would get some cough syrup. Kyla went to her tent for a sponge bath.

Kibo had left a pot of hot water inside. Kyla lit her lantern and threw her sweater, T-shirt and pants into a heap in the corner. Her underwear went next and she stood naked and shivering as she sponged hot water over her body. She felt cleaner and more invigorated with every stroke.

Chase could see her shadow on the side of the tent. He thought he had his emotions under control, but the outline of her upturned breasts, flat stomach and long legs set his heart pounding like a jackhammer in his chest.

He tried to pretend it was an ordinary male response to an ordinary female, brought on because he was accustomed to seeing that certain female in shapeless hiking clothes. But if Kyla was an ordinary female, then he was Edmund Hillary on his way to the top of Everest for the first time. He tried to walk on by to his own tent, where he, too, would strip down and wash off the accumulation of two days' worth of dirt, but he stood fixed to the spot.

Her movements were graceful, and he couldn't tear his eyes away. He wanted to go in, take the sponge out of her hand and throw it aside. He would hold the soap in his hands and start at the top of her shoulders, then slide his hands down...

She was drying off now, and he finally summoned the willpower to go to his own tent. What do you want? he asked himself, scrubbing off a layer of skin in his zeal. A guide who is part geisha and part superwoman? No, he told himself, while he rubbed himself dry. He only wanted Kyla. But he thought she was more than he deserved and more than he was going to get, if that "Keep off" look on her face was any indication.

That look had softened by the time they'd finished bathing and he met her at the trailhead. Or maybe it was just the moonlight shining on her clean hair and face. He couldn't decide.

"You smell good," she said inhaling appreciatively.

He took her hand. "And you look like the goddess Lakshmi glowing in the dark."

She laughed and they followed Kibo across the clearing and into the woods, still holding hands. "Lakshmi doesn't glow by herself," she explained. "Her way is lighted with lamps."

He tightened his grip, rubbing her palm with his thumb. "Kibo is lighting your way with his lantern. Is that good enough?"

"Good enough for me, but not for Lakshmi. People clean their houses for her and strew them with garlands of flowers, if they want prosperity for the year to come."

"That's fair. What would you bestow on me if I cleaned my tent and strewed it with flowers?" he asked, pulling her close to him. They continued down the trail in silence, their eyes on the lantern swinging hypnotically ahead of them in the dark. He began to wonder if she'd heard him.

"I couldn't guarantee prosperity," she answered finally.

"I'm not asking for any guarantees," he said, his voice deep.

"Oh, Chase." It was a plea from the heart and he wished he had never started this conversation.

"Forget it. I'm sorry. There's something I don't understand, isn't there? Something I don't know about you."

"Yes," she admitted, seeing the lights of the village flickering through the trees.

Kibo led them to the Thakuri family, who stood at the door of their house and ranged in age from about eighty to a few months. *"Namaste,"* they cried.

Chase and Kyla pressed their hands together and lowered their heads. *"Namaste,"* they responded together. Instantly they were surrounded by giggling children, and their parents beamed a warm welcome to the guests of honor as they led them inside. What little furniture there was had been pushed against the walls, making a large space for everyone to sit on the floor. With rice grains and bright powders, the family had already drawn one sacred circle, a mandala, for each member and one for Yama, the king of death.

Chase exchanged a glance with Kyla. "I'll sit next to the raj's circle," he volunteered.

She shook her head. "I'm not afraid of death. There's no death without life."

Her words startled him. Were they the key that would unlock the mystery of Kyla Tanner? Her secret gnawed at him. He stared at her, trying to see beneath the surface—the smooth face, the windblown hair and the smoke-gray eyes. When would she trust him enough to tell him?

A little girl toddled over to Kyla, her small hands clutching a tray of fruits and nuts. She tripped on the hem of her silk sari and showered Kyla with raisins, sunflower seeds, almonds and dried figs. The wide-eyed child burst into tears and Kyla hugged her until she stopped crying and settled quietly in Kyla's lap, her mouth full of raisins.

Kyla smoothed back the little girl's straight black hair and retied her red ribbon, and an unfamiliar longing filled her heart. She knew Chase was looking at her. She could feel the heat of his gaze, almost hear him say, "I told you so. It feels right, doesn't it, to hold a child in your arms?" She couldn't deny it. The weight of the small body, the soft skin and the lingering smell of babyhood combined to evoke a bittersweet feeling that pierced her heart.

Then the real food came: platters of chicken and rice and round flatbread smeared with yak butter. Kyla tore off small pieces for the child in her lap and accepted a glass of *raksi* for herself. It burned her throat as it went down and left her feeling relaxed, as if she might never move again.

Across the room Chase lifted his glass in a silent toast and she remembered the night at the Yak and Yeti when she'd spilled her wine at the sight of him across the crowded restaurant. He had the power, with one gesture, to set her on fire, or was she just feeling the effects of the potent rice wine? She smiled tentatively and he smiled back, holding her gaze. A big bowl filled with flower petals was passed around. The little girl sprinkled them over Kyla's head and shoulders and still she was held by the look in Chase's eyes. She had never been in love before, never felt she couldn't live without someone, never known that pain and ecstasy could coexist the way life and death did.

If this was it, then she finally understood what all the songs and poetry were about. But in songs and stories love lasted forever. This love would last twenty-four days and then disappear into the thin air at twelve thousand feet just as fast as it had appeared somewhere in the steamy valley of Kathmandu.

She stood, suddenly realizing that the party was over. And then they were out in the street, calling their thanks and best wishes through the dark to the noisy, laughing family group hanging about their front door.

Chase put his arm around Kyla's shoulders and held her tightly. They walked down the trail that way, shoulder to shoulder, hip to hip. Did he know she loved him? Did he care? Had she fallen in love with someone who didn't love her? Did it matter? She wanted to laugh, she wanted to cry, she wanted to tell someone. She wanted to tell Chase, but she wouldn't. She couldn't until she'd told him everything else first. And that was out of the question.

"I'm glad we went" was all she said.

"You looked glad." He tightened his grip on her. "You looked beautiful. Festivals suit you. You should go to one every day."

"Why?" she asked. "To look beautiful?"

"To look happy, relaxed, soft, warm..." His voice deepened until it turned into a caress. They stopped walking, and Chase looked at her until she pulled away from him and ran down the path. She was so close to telling him how she felt, and that scared her—scared her so much, she didn't stop running until she threw herself into her tent and pulled the sleeping bag up over her head.

She could hear Kibo rustling around with pots and pans, coughing in the distance, then voices, Kibo's and Chase's. They were walking back and forth between Chase's tent and the porter's. Kyla sat up, trying to hear what was going on.

The flaps of her tent parted and Chase stuck his head inside. "Kibo spilled kerosene all over my tent."

"Oh, no."

"Oh, yes. He was filling the lamp. It's mopped up now but there's this awful smell in there."

"You can't sleep in there."

"No, I'll sleep outside. It's not that cold."

"There's room in here."

"I was hoping you'd say that." He disappeared just as fast as he'd arrived and was back a minute later with his sleeping bag. He spread it out next to Kyla and slid into its warm depths. He shifted to his side, propped his head on his hand and looked at her. But the soft, relaxed expression on her face had gone. He didn't know if she wanted him in there or not.

"I wonder if we could back up a little," he said quietly. "We were having a conversation out there on the trail and you left rather abruptly."

"I had a cramp," she answered quickly.

"Where? In your side?"

"No, in my foot."

"You made pretty good speed for someone with a cramp in her foot."

"It's gone now," she assured him.

"Good. It was a nice festival, don't you think?"

"Very nice. But I'm going to sleep now."

He reached out and touched her hair that was spilling out of her sleeping bag. She moved away from him. He sighed loudly.

"I can't sleep," he told her.

She turned over. "Why don't you close your eyes…and your mouth?"

He grinned. "I feel wired. That's what festivals do to me." He was rewarded with a small smile that she tried to smother. "What do you do at night with your group?" he asked.

"We go to sleep."

"I mean before that, when you're all too excited to sleep. Do you provide back rubs or massages?" he suggested hopefully.

She closed her eyes. "Sometimes we tell stories around the campfire."

He looked at her profile—at her long eyelashes and straight nose, her lips and throat—and he could barely control his longing to touch her, to take her in his arms and hold her.

"But you're too tired to tell stories tonight, aren't you?" he said.

She nodded and turned away from him. And suddenly she was asleep while he lay watching her wondering why she'd run away from him on the path; why she always ran from any encounter with him.

In the morning Chase was awakened by the banging of pots in the porter's tent. Reluctantly he sat up and rubbed his eyes. Sleeping so close to Kyla was agony. She sighed in her sleep but didn't move. Yesterday had been a long day, and he hoped she would sleep late today. The sun made a halo over the dome of the tent and he wanted to stay there forever, to keep the world at bay and create an island of safety and security. But he could no more hold Kyla captive in a tent than he could capture a hummingbird restless with energy and drive.

Outside Kibo was making breakfast and packing up, and somewhere beyond were children who would go blind if he didn't reach them before the passes closed for the winter.

He raked his hands through his hair, then quietly edged his way through the flaps of the tent. The wide, grassy meadow was wet with dew sparkling in the early-morning sunshine. There was a bite to the air that made him think of fall and home. Some day he might even go home, to autumn and falling leaves and cool, crisp weather. But he didn't want to go anywhere without Kyla; he wanted to be wherever she was. How that would work out after this trip, with Kyla on a raft on the Yangtze River and himself removing cataracts in an operating room, he didn't know.

When Kyla finally awoke, it took her only seconds to realize that she'd overslept, and even less time to roll up her sleeping bag and lace up her boots. The dry, cold air meant they were getting closer to their destination. A pang of sadness went through her. After they distributed the vitamins, they would have no further reason to be together.

Kyla could admit to herself that she was in love with Chase, but she knew it was her secret to keep, along with the other secret that she kept from the world. They must finish this trip as they'd started—as friends, no more, no less. It wasn't going to be easy, but there was no other way.

When she stepped outside, she found breakfast ready. She ate her omelet in silence and tried not to think about having slept next to Chase all night. She knew the reason she'd slept so well and so long was that she'd felt peaceful and secure with him next to her.

"How did you sleep?" he asked, as if he'd read her mind.

She took a last sip of tea, then hooked her metal cup to the outside strap of her backpack. "Fine," she answered brightly. "But tonight you'll have your own tent back and more room to, uh, stretch out."

"I've already talked to Kibo about that," he said, watching him wash the pans at the edge of the stream. "He agrees that it would save time if he only had to set up one tent at night." He shrugged indifferently. "I actually had plenty of room. What about you?"

She nodded. Plenty of room but not plenty of resistance. How many nights could she spend next to him without it getting to be a habit—a dangerous habit she would have a hard time breaking?

On the other hand, how could she sleep by herself, thinking about him lying a few yards away and missing his warm breath on her cheek, his hands on her hair? He was waiting for her answer.

"We might be staying in a monastery tonight," she suggested. "So we won't have to use the tents at all."

"A monastery?"

She nodded. "I don't know if we'll get that far today, but the monks of Senge Yeshe reserve rooms for pilgrims."

"Is that what we are?"

"No, but if there are no pilgrims, we'll be allowed to use the space and they'll feed us yak stew and yogurt."

He tried to smile, but his heart sank. No tent, no island of security with the two of them alone together.

She saw the downcast look on his face. "It's good, believe me. The stew simmers for days, and they make their own bread and fermented rice drink. If we get there by nightfall, you'll appreciate a bed and a hot meal."

"I'm sure I will," he assured her, and tightened the laces on his boots for the long climb ahead.

They didn't seen Annapurna until after they had climbed steep rock ridges that plunged to the valley floor, and passed old men knitting sweaters with umbrella spokes. Suddenly Kyla stopped and waited for Chase to catch up to her. She pointed to the mountains rising above them.

Nothing had prepared him for the sharp rise of the peaks, the white pyramids that seemed to shoot up from the clouds. He looked down at Kyla's face uplifted to the sky. Her eyes were shining with tears.

She smiled sheepishly. "Don't mind me. I always cry when I see Annapurna or Everest or Himalchuli."

Chase nodded understandingly. "I've climbed the Sierras and the Tetons, but this is spectacular." Her gaze was fixed on the distant mountain and he knew this was not the time to ask her what she thought about a future together. There was time. Twenty-one more days.

It was almost dusk when they glimpsed the high lama of the monastery sitting on the edge of a cliff, chanting prayers with the sun setting behind him. Kyla gave Chase a triumphant smile.

"We're making good time." She pointed to a row of orange-robed monks in the distance, blowing on long horns. The monks stared straight ahead as Kyla and Chase walked by, and continued beating on their yak-hide drums.

Inside the whitewashed monastery, a novice showed them to their quarters. Chase was disappointed to see there were plenty of rooms. The young monk explained that there had been no pilgrims since spring, but only two days ago they had accommodated another trekker, the famous Colonel Prajapati and his group, bound for the Annapurna sanctuary.

Kyla set down her pack on the rough-hewn boards of the floor. "He didn't tell me he was coming up here. It's lucky we didn't all arrive at once. We would have had to share a room again."

The monk disappeared with a low bow and Chase dropped his pack next to Kyla's. "What was so bad about that?" he asked with a grin. "As I recall, you slept like a log."

"No, I didn't," she protested.

"Well, you didn't move a muscle."

"That's because I didn't want to wake you up."

"I was awake all night." He leaned against the wall and looked at her. "I was thinking about this trip." He trailed one finger down her jaw and under her chin.

"Is it what you thought it would be?" she asked.

"I thought we'd head off and after some strenuous walking we'd be in the Manang Valley handing out vitamins. I didn't think about what would happen in between—to you, to me…to us." His finger found her mouth and traced the outline of her lips. "It's the biggest adventure of my life."

Her lips parted. "Me, too," she whispered.

"You?" he asked.

"Yes. I thought I'd seen everything and done everything. But it's different with you along, seeing things through your eyes…." She turned and opened the door to her room. "I don't know why that is," she said as an afterthought.

He followed her inside the small, narrow cubicle and watched her sit on the edge of the straw mattress covered with a rough cloth bedspread. "I know why, and so do you. We both feel it and it keeps getting stronger." Her face paled in the flickering light from the gas lamp on the wall. Her eyes looked huge and alarmed, but he continued. "I'm not going to push you or ask you to do anything about it, but I want to tell you that you're important to me and I have no intention of letting you go anywhere without me."

A small smile tugged at the corners of her mouth. "Well, that's going to be interesting, trying to find a place for you in my dugout canoe on the Amazon next spring."

He smiled back. "I've always wanted to go up the Amazon. They could probably use some vitamin A tablets there, too."

Her smile faded as she realized he was serious. "Chase, do you know what my job is really like?"

He leaned against the wall. "I think so. I've met one of your groups, heard the stories of how you cook whole goats over spits, rescue frightened hikers from swaying bridges. And now I'm seeing it for myself, firsthand."

She sighed and tucked her legs underneath her. "Yes, but you're only seeing the fun and excitement. What really happens is that I spend hours organizing these trips, with a calculator and a map and an almanac. Then, when we actually hit the trail, all ten of us, there are tensions, arguments, attractions and the kinds of circumstances that bring out the worst in people. It's hard to imagine, I know. With just the two of us we can do what we like, make last-minute changes, stay up all night and sleep late in the morning. But with a group, it's not that flexible."

He stared at her. "You mean you're having a better time with me than you usually do with a whole group?"

She smiled at the incredulous look on his face. "Of course I am. I thought you knew that. I'm having a great time. The festival, the baby we helped deliver—I've never had such a good time in my life.'' She beamed at him and she suddenly knew it was true. Sharing this trip with Chase was an entirely different experience from sharing it with nine strangers.

''Neither have I,'' he said quietly.

Far away the monastery bells began to ring, calling the monks to prayer, and Kyla had a sinking feeling that she hadn't discouraged Chase at all; that all she'd done was to convince him even more than ever that this trip was just the beginning for them, and not the end.

Chapter Eight

At dinner that night they ate at long narrow tables with the orange-robed monks, and the yak stew was just as good as Kyla had promised. Certainly she hadn't frightened Chase off. Instead he was more determined than ever to make her part of his life, part of his future. But the bare, ascetic monastery was not the place to talk about it. He wanted to be out under the stars, lying next to her in a grassy meadow or in a tent where there was no place to hide, no place to run but into his arms.

After dinner they went to their separate rooms and Chase tossed and turned just as he'd done at the Himalayan View Hotel, but for different reasons. Then he couldn't sleep with her next to him. Now he couldn't sleep without her. While he was trying to think up an excuse to go into her room, there was a knock on his door. "Come in," he said, hoping it was Kyla.

It was. She was barefoot and shivering despite the long underwear that clung to every curve like a second skin. She wrapped her arms around her waist. "I think I saw a bat."

"Where? In your room?"

"No, no. Outside." She looked around. "Do you want me to close your window?"

"I'm not cold." He pulled his sleeping bag up over his chin. He wanted to unzip it, open his arms and take her in with him, but he didn't. This time she would have to make the first move. "Maybe it was a bird," he suggested.

"Birds don't fly at night." She padded lightly to the window and looked out to see a black object come swooping out of the night sky and fly straight at her. She threw herself on top of Chase, burying her head in his chest. The bat flew into the room and circled wildly, frantically looking for a way out.

Chase shifted his body so he could slide out of the sleeping bag, and carefully zipped Kyla in. When the bat slowed down, he trapped it in a corner, holding it gently in his hands. He let it go out the window. Then he closed the window and sat at the foot of the bed.

"You can look out now, it's gone."

She peered out over the edge of the sleeping bag. "Thank you."

"Are you afraid of bats?" he asked. "Or were you just looking for an excuse to come in and see me?"

She sat up straight. "That's the most outrageous thing I've ever heard." She pulled her knees up to her chin and swung out of the bag.

He moved quickly to hold her by the arms. "Just a minute. Maybe I can help you the way you helped me over the bridge."

"It's not the same thing. I wasn't frightened of a bat when I was a child. It's just that I'm afraid they'll get tangled in my hair. There's nothing strange about that."

He shook his head at her ignorance. Then he lifted her legs and put her back into his sleeping bag.

"Wait a minute," she protested. "I'm not staying."

"You're staying until we give bats a fair hearing," he said, leaning forward, his hands on the mattress, on either side of her shoulders.

She exhaled and relaxed. The bat was gone. She was in Chase's sleeping bag where the warmth of his body still lingered. They were on a safe subject—not her, not him, just bats. She smiled up at him and he leaned over to graze her lips with his.

"Go on," she urged.

"With what?" he asked, kissing the hollow in her throat.

"The hearing," she murmured breathlessly.

"That's right." He kissed her again on the lips and within him the fire he'd been so carefully tending burst into flames.

She brought her arms out and held his face in her hands to gaze into his dark eyes. He kissed the palms of her hands and she pulled his face to hers, wanting to be crushed against him, to feel the hard muscles under his soft flannel shirt.

There were footsteps in the hall, the soft padding of a monk's hemp slippers. Kyla froze and an irrepressible urge to giggle threatened to give them away. Chase shook his head and clamped his hand over her mouth.

When the footsteps had faded, he grinned down at her and whispered, "Where were we?"

"I've got to get back to my room. What if they check?"

"You haven't heard about bats yet." He blocked her way with his body. "Even though they're almost blind, they can't get tangled in your hair." He paused and ran his hands through her brown curls. "Because they navigate by sonar."

"Is that right?" she whispered, thinking only of his fingers in her hair.

"They're mammals, you know. Flying mammals related to mice."

She shivered. "Mice? You don't think there are mice here, do you?"

"Do you mean you're afraid of mice, too? Come on, I'll carry you back to your room." He lifted her, sleeping bag and all, and opened the door with one hand. Kyla buried her head in his shoulder.

Chase set her on her bed, then took her sleeping bag with him. "You stay in mine, right where you are. I'll use yours."

He was gone before she could protest or thank him or apologize. She lay thinking about his lips on hers, the weight of his body against her. It must have been his sleeping bag around her, reminding her of him, the smell of smoke and pine and the cold, clear air of the Himalayas. And then there was the disturbing image of a dugout canoe somewhere on the Amazon with Kyla, a group of adventure travelers and one doctor with a large duffel bag full of medical equipment.

She should not go to Chase's room at night, bats or no bats. She should not discuss the future with him, ever. But something happened to her control when Chase was around. Just a look or a touch, and her reserve melted. She would have to be more careful from now on. She had a goal—to get Chase to the Manang Valley. Then she could get on with her life. And he could get on with his. Her intrusion into his life distracted him, whether he realized it or not.

He said he wouldn't let her go anywhere without him, but she knew that high altitude could affect one's judgment. Chase might have a slight case of altitude sickness. He showed signs of random, illogical thinking and light-headedness. She might have a touch of it herself, which would explain why she went to Chase's room tonight. She turned over and buried her head in his sleeping bag and inhaled the smell of the soap he used and the flannel shirt he wore. She squeezed her eyes shut and concentrated on mountain climbing.

At breakfast the monks told them the snows were falling in the upper peaks. Kyla and Chase exchanged glances and vowed to make better time.

For four days they pushed themselves onward and upward. They bought a yak to help carry the extra supplies. The animal scrambled ahead of them and inspired them with his surefooted agility. They camped in fields that offered spectacular vistas, but they were almost too tired to look, and fell into dreamless sleep each night.

Chase had a headache every morning. But the dizziness he felt from the altitude was usually gone by the time they had their first cup of tea, and he could breathe in the clean cold air with a rush of pleasure. Today, part of the pleasure was seeing Kyla's cheeks turn pink and her eyes glow.

She put her jacket on and snapped it close under her chin. "Kibo wants us to stay in his village tonight, in the home of the tigers."

"If you're afraid of bats, how are you going to face these tigers?"

She raised her chin and smiled at him. "The Sherpa climbers are called the tigers of the snow because they're so strong, and they've been carrying goods over these passes for generations. And I'm not afraid of bats. Not really."

"Then you did come in to see *me* that night."

Kyla turned to pat the bulging saddlebags hanging on either side of the yak's broad back, but not before he saw her face redden at the memory of that night.

She didn't answer, and they were on the trail again, a steep switchback made of fitted stones smoothed by innumerable footsteps. Dark clouds hid the higher peaks and Kibo predicted strong winds and possible snow flurries.

By midafternoon they reached Kibo's village, with its thirty or more houses arranged horseshoe-shape on a sharply rising hillside. Kibo's sister and mother and wife met them at the door of the guesthouse with hot tea, flinging questions at him in their native dialect. Then they were gone, taking Kibo with them and leaving behind a fire in the hearth with an iron pot swinging above it.

The wind rattled the narrow windows and Chase moved to the fire and held out his hands. He followed Kyla's gaze to the loft suspended from the rafters by thick ropes.

"You want to sleep up there, don't you?"

She took off her jacket and stood with her back to the fire. "Do you always know what I'm thinking?"

He sat on a straight-backed chair, rubbed his hands and stared into the flames. "I wish I did. So I'll know if you believe this trip is something truly special, something extra wonderful."

"This trip is like no other, believe me." Her voice sounded tired. "But it will also end. Then I'll be riding a canoe in the Amazon and you'll be back in your hospital." She said the words so firmly, as though she were issuing a command.

Chase looked at her for a long time. He could think of no right response. Finally Kibo knocked at the door with a pan of hot water. Chase invited her to bathe first by waving his arm at the steaming pot, then grabbed his jacket and went outside.

He took a long walk around the village, trying not to think of Kyla sponging off in the tiny guesthouse. Children, gathering green firewood, waved and called to him. He thought about bringing children into the world—his own children—and he wondered if Kyla would ever change her mind. He had heard what she'd said—that there was no room in her life for him—and he knew that she meant it. He sat on a rock behind the houses and dropped his head in his hands. The wind came down off the mountains and blew the warmth out of his body until he felt more alone than he ever had before.

When he went back to the little hut it was empty. Then Kibo appeared with another pot of hot water and told him to come to his mother's house when he'd finished his bath. There he would find the memsahib.

By the time Chase walked into Kibo's mother's stone hut, Kyla was already wedged in the place of honor between Kibo's sister and his wife. A glass of chang was in her hand. The sight of his clean-shaven face and his smile as he greeted the hosts made her heart turn over. It was warm in the tiny house, and Kyla's cheeks flamed when Chase caught her eye. She was grateful for the noise, for the people and the celebration, for anything to keep some distance between them.

He had come very close to wearing her down, to convincing her to take a chance and tell him the truth. Somehow she had to find the strength to resist him, to convince him that her job was the most important thing in the world to her. She knew she was right, but when he looked at her and held her in his arms, she wanted to reach for the stars. Reaching was all right; it was coming up empty-handed that scared her—scared her so much that she found herself shaking just thinking of taking a chance on happiness. She had made up her mind long ago to live a normal life for as long as she could, and take the consequences. Now there was someone she wanted to share the consequences with.

A new barrel of chang was carried into the room and someone handed Kyla a bowl of potato soup and grain cakes fried in oil. Someone else showed her where to sit. That was next to Chase at the dining table.

"What's the celebration this time?" he asked, so close that she smelled the soap he washed with and saw pinpoints of light in the depths of his dark eyes.

She dipped her spoon carefully into her soup. "A homecoming for Kibo."

He looked around the room. "Where are all the men?"

"Trekking. It's good because it brings money to the village. But it's bad because it divides the families."

"So it's because of us Kibo is separated from his wife and family."

"Yes, but it's because of us he'll be able to buy them a pair of goats this summer, and some day a generator or a well."

"I saw some kids cutting firewood outside."

"I feel bad about that."

"Why? It's not your fault. You use a stove."

"But not all trekkers do. The slopes we passed today used to be covered with trees. That's what Kibo's grandmother told me," she said. "The mountains look like they'll last forever, but actually they're much more fragile." She peered out the window into the darkness as if she might catch a glimpse of Annapurna.

"They remind me of someone I know," he murmured.

Kyla felt her cheeks burn and she cut a grain cake into small pieces.

"A very fragile environment, subject to erosion because of lack of nurturing," he continued.

"I'm talking about mountains," she reminded him.

"Isn't it true that the Sherpas were better off before the trekkers came along?" he asked. "What if one guide quit trekking, quit bringing groups up here and did something else with her life? Think what it would do for the environment."

She sipped her tea. "I don't think it would make that much difference. Besides," she warned under her breath, "I love this life. I'm not giving it up."

They didn't speak after that.

When the meal was over, the songs and dances began, and everyone shifted toward the makeshift stage in the middle of the room. The women locked arms and formed a line, stepping forward and then backward in time to their singing. The rhythmic music and the hot tea lulled Kyla into a drowsy contentment. Her eyelids were heavy and in danger of closing. She felt Chase's hand on the back of her neck.

"Time for bed," he whispered, and guided her out through the crowded room with his hand on her elbow.

The cold air shocked her into full alertness just as she was about to link arms with Chase. Instead she walked carefully across the bare field to the guesthouse, her hands deep in her pockets. Inside, she took her pack and climbed the stepladder to the loft, leaving Chase standing in the center of the floor looking up at her.

"I'm sorry," he said. "I won't suggest you give up your work again."

She spread out her sleeping bag and looked down at him.

"I'm sorry, too." She swallowed hard. "I appreciate your concern for the environment, and for me. But you know how I feel. It makes it hard...." She buried her face in her sleeping bag.

He put his foot on the bottom rung of the ladder. "I know it does. So I won't say any more about it. But if you change your mind, make sure you tell me. You know where to find me."

She looked up. "Down there on that mattress in the corner?"

He nodded. Then he knelt on the floor and found the sulfa tablets in the bottom of his pack. He poured himself a cup of water from the barrel on the table and swallowed the medicine, hoping his headache would be gone by morning.

"What are you doing?" Kyla leaned over the edge of the loft, her hair falling forward in a tangle of curls.

"Taking a pill."

"What for?"

He swore under his breath. He should have waited until she fell asleep. "Just a headache."

"You didn't eat much at dinner," she remarked. "How come?"

"Not hungry."

She leaned over farther until he was afraid she would fall onto the firewood stacked below her. "Headache, loss of appetite, what else?" she demanded.

"Nausea and dizziness," he admitted, lying on his back on the rough-hewn floor and closing his eyes as the interior of the hut reeled around.

He heard her come down. "Why didn't you tell me you have altitude sickness?" She put her cool hand on his forehead.

"Didn't want to slow us down," he mumbled. "I'll be all right in the morning."

"We're not going anywhere in the morning." She lifted his head onto her lap and he felt the soft fabric of her thermal underwear, but he was too sick to do anything about it. Maybe they weren't going anywhere in the morning.

With her arms around him, he stumbled to his bed. She propped his head on a pillow and brought him a glass of water. "You have to force fluids. Your body's losing tremendous amounts of liquid in this dry air. And if you don't eat you won't have the strength to go anywhere."

"I can't eat now," he protested. "I'm sorry about this."

"It's my fault." Her fingers gently traced the outline of his face. "I'm usually good at spotting these things, even with nine trekkers in my group. How come I missed you?"

He shifted to his side as waves of dizziness hit him. "I wanted you to miss me. You're the guide, I'm the doctor. I'll take care of it."

"I've seen more cases of altitude sickness than you have," she insisted. "I know what to do. There's no reason to be ashamed. It can happen to anyone, even marathon runners and professional athletes. It has to do with how well your body acclimatizes."

He forced his eyes open. "My body acclimatizes fine. I've been to the Rockies and the Sierras and I've never been sick before."

"You forget that the Himalayas begin where other mountains stop. We're up very high and we've come up fairly fast. Tomorrow we rest. After that we'll see how you feel."

He felt her unlacing his boots, then removing his heavy socks. "I'm not helpless," he said.

"Can you get your pants off by yourself?" she asked.

He considered the question from his hazy perspective, and shook his head.

"Don't be embarrassed," she told him. "We're just doctor and patient here." Her fingers deftly unzipped his pants and her hands grazed the sides of his legs as she pulled his trousers off, leaving him in his long underwear. His heart pounded, but it was not a symptom of altitude sickness. If only he didn't feel so rotten. If only he could open his eyes and see the look on her face. But if he did, he'd also see the room spinning around him and he couldn't risk that.

He felt her wrap a cotton sheet around him, then his sleeping bag over that, like a quilt. She leaned forward. "If you need anything," she whispered, "you know where to find me."

He nodded and dozed off. When he woke up she was not in the loft above him. He felt a panic rising in his throat. Kyla was not where she was supposed to be. There was a pale gray light coming through the window and he knew it was morning. And she was gone. He sat up and his head pounded.

Then she came through the door and his world fell into place again. Her red wool hat matched her flushed cheeks and she carried a basket covered with a handwoven cloth.

"How do you feel?" She sat on the edge of the bed and brushed the hair off his forehead.

"Better, now that you're here. Where were you, Little Red Riding Hood?"

"Getting you some food. You need carbohydrates."

He sat up and put his arms around her. "I need more than that. I need sympathy. I need a companion."

She held the basket over her head. "Watch out, you'll smash the buckwheat cakes." Then she put the basket down, smeared honey on a pancake and placed it carefully in his mouth.

He chewed and swallowed. "What time is it? We've got to get going."

"We're resting today, remember?" She stood and poured hot water from the iron pot on the hearth to make tea.

"We can't afford to rest." He swung his legs over the side of the bed and stared at his long underwear.

"We can't afford not to. They say men are terrible patients, and doctors are the worst."

"I don't remember taking my pants off," he said with a frown.

She handed him a cup of tea. "You didn't. I did."

"Then you'll have to put them back on me, because we're leaving today."

"Chase, I'll give them to you when you're ready to travel. Maybe you feel better, but you still look terrible." She realized that despite his shaggy hair and the dark stubble on his chin, he couldn't ever really look terrible. She stood over him, her gaze traveling over his face. His eyes were half closed, his face drained of color. She held the teacup to his lips and he drank some. Then she lifted his long legs back onto the bed.

He kicked the sheet off his feet. "What are we going to do all day?" he asked. "We can't just lie around."

"I'm going to do some mending and some writing. And you're going to lie right there. Didn't you bring any medical journals to read?"

"They're boring. They don't apply to me. They're for doctors in hospitals with dialysis machines and CAT scanners. I only do the most basic stuff. As you know." He yawned and closed his eyes. He had to rest, but it was maddening, frustrating. He would never again order bed rest for a patient without feeling a pang of sympathy. He fought off drowsiness. If he fell asleep Kyla might leave again and never come back.

"Come here," he said, his voice thick with fatigue. He heard her footsteps and felt the pressure of her hand on his.

"What is it?"

"Don't leave."

"No, I won't. I'll be right here."

He sighed and felt her light kiss on his cheek. Then he fell asleep.

Chapter Nine

It might have been hours or even days later when Chase struggled back to consciousness. The sky was dark gray outside the narrow windows and Kyla sat on a bench in the corner under the gas lamp writing in a spiral notebook. Her legs were folded under her and he could hear her pencil scratching against the paper. That and the crackling of the fire were the only sounds in the little hut.

His head was heavy, his throat dry as he lay watching her. Maybe they could stay here forever, forget about time, dispense whatever medicine he had left, and live a simple life growing potatoes. He smiled at the thought. She looked up over her notebook and smiled back.

He wanted to hold the moment forever, have it frozen in time: the lamplight on her hair, the soft curve of her cheek, the slow movement as she set her book down and poured him some tea.

The sweet, hot drink soothed his throat. "I guess I slept."

"I guess you did—about eight hours."

He shook his head in disbelief and she handed him a bowl of light brown mush. He wrinkled his forehead, but ate it. Kyla smiled encouragingly.

"What were you writing?" he asked.

She picked up the notebook and drew the chair up to the solid wooden table. "My journal. I had a lot of catching up to do."

"What do you put in there?" He set his bowl down and leaned back against the wall.

"The route we took, the weather, any problems. I shouldn't have let it go. Now I can't remember where we were two nights ago."

He rubbed his head. "At the monastery?"

"No, not the monastery. I remember the monastery."

"So do I. I remember you coming into my room in your long underwear. Did you write about that?"

She looked down at her book and he couldn't tell if she was smiling. He folded his arms behind his head. "Two nights ago... Was that the first night we slept together in the tent?"

"No," she said, her eyes still on the book. "That was a long time ago."

"A long, long time ago," he agreed. "It seems like I've known you forever. No wonder you had such a hard time saying goodbye to your group."

There was a long silence. The water in the pot boiled and Kyla lifted the lid. "It's the trek through the mountains. It's sharing experiences that brings people together. The path becomes the trail of life with all the ups and downs."

Chase leaned forward. "You and I are on that trail together right now. Our goal is the Manang Valley, but the climb is just as important. The goal isn't what life's about, either. It's about the process of getting there."

Kyla dipped her cup into the pot. "Let's not get carried away with this. Here on the trail I know the way so I can show it to you. But on the trail of life there are no guides. No one's been on your trip before, and no one's been on mine, so they can't tell us which way to go. We each have to find our own separate way."

Chase stretched his legs. "Yes, but our separate ways are merging, don't you feel that?"

She set down her cup. "For now, maybe. But our goals are different. That's the wonderful thing about travel. We pass a lot of places and meet a lot of strangers, and when the trip is over we leave them behind. But they're always a part of us in our memories."

"Are memories good enough for you, Kyla?"

She studied her hands. "Yes, but I'm lucky. I always start another trip with new people, a new goal and a new route. That way I pack a lot of different lives into one lifetime. Not many people can do that." She met his gaze, daring him to contradict her.

His headache stretched across his forehead. "Is that what you're going to do?"

"Of course. That's my job. That's my life."

"Do you mean nothing's changed? This trip hasn't meant anything to you? What about everything we shared together? I don't understand you."

She vigorously stirred the sugar into her tea, clanking her spoon against the sides of the cup. "That's because you don't listen to me."

"I listened when you said this was a trip like no other. But maybe that's just what you tell everyone..." He couldn't stop bitterness from creeping into his voice.

Turning her back to him, she knelt down at the stone fireplace. "It's never been this way before," she said softly. "It's my fault. I should have known better. It started the first day I saw you." With a poker she pulled out the potatoes that had been roasting in the coals.

He smiled. "The day you tried to bribe me to admit Lillian into the hospital... Aren't you ashamed of yourself?"

"I didn't like you. I couldn't stand you. I thought you were the most arrogant, the most self-centered, egotistical doctor...." She paused to put the food on plates and looked around for the utensils.

He lifted his legs and they felt heavy, as if he'd never be able to use them again. "What made you change your mind? Or have you?"

She set one plate with a potato and a fork on his lap. "I don't know. Maybe it was that night at the Yak and Yeti when I saw you eating alone. I can't stand to see people eat alone." She sat on the end of his bed with her plate on her lap, and folded her legs under her. She took a bite of the steaming potato.

"Is that why you sent that guy in your group over to get me?"

Her fork clattered to her plate. "I never sent anyone to get you. That was entirely his idea. You were certainly eager to come. What do you do—go to those places so you can meet Americans?"

He grinned at her. "That's right. I go there every night, hoping some loudmouthed American tourists will invite me to eat with them so we can talk about home. Believe it or not, some people like to eat alone."

"Then why did you come over?"

"I honestly thought you had sent him."

She felt a shiver go up her spine. "Did you really?"

"I didn't want to hurt your feelings."

She studied his face, pale beneath his tan, and the lines that forked out around his eyes, and her chest tightened.

She looked down at her plate, then at his. "Eat. You need the carbohydrates."

He took a bite and chewed. "You haven't changed. You're still trying to tell me what to do."

"Then, why—"

"Why did I hire you to be my guide?" He shook his head. "I don't know. I thought you were overbearing, and I didn't know how to get rid of you. I thought if I made you help out in the operating room you might leave. But something else happened. I got used to having you there handing me the instruments. I liked seeing you in the morning and I missed you in the afternoon when you weren't around."

Kyla tried to smile, but the corners of her mouth wouldn't turn up. She pressed her lips together and her eyes stung with tears.

He dug into the potato with his fork. "Believe me, getting mixed up with some hard-headed woman was not in my plans. But then you volunteered to take me on this trip. I couldn't believe my luck."

"And here we are," she said softly.

"Here we are," he echoed, reaching for her hands. Then his eyes closed and Kyla stood at the side of his bed looking down at him. He opened his eyes and squinted at her. "Don't leave me."

"I won't." She wouldn't leave him until they'd done what they set out to do. But after that she would go, and he knew it.

Satisfied, he closed his eyes again.

Kyla put her journal away and picked up Chase's shirt to sew up a rip he'd made climbing over a rock the day before. She was lucky, she told herself, to have so much to look forward to. Chase had a full life before she walked into his hospital, and he would always have his work. And if that wasn't enough, there were women who would fall in love with him, someone who would be willing to follow him to strange places, to hand him instruments and help him deliver babies.

She pricked her finger and a drop of blood fell on his dark flannel shirt. Chase with someone else. It was something she didn't want to think about. She pressed her finger against her palm to stop the bleeding. Why shouldn't someone else have him if she wouldn't? He was the most unselfish man she'd ever known, and he deserved the best: someone who would care for him as much as he cared for her, someone who had a full life to look forward to, someone who could have children and raise them. The sooner Kyla got out of his life the sooner he could get on with it.

She crawled up to her loft and leaned over to watch him sleep. She had no pictures of him. She didn't want any. It would be hard enough to forget about him with just her memories. She pulled her sleeping bag over her eyes and waited for dawn.

Chase had wanted to leave in the morning. His head had seemed light, as if it had been floating somewhere above his body, but his headache had gone. He'd felt tired, but he hadn't told Kyla. Somehow she'd known and had not let them go.

At dusk Kibo put a small golden statue of Buddha and two candles on the table and lit the candles. Kyla fed Chase more baked potatoes, and when he protested, she sat on the edge of his bed with a fork in her hand.

"We're leaving tomorrow," he told her firmly.

"Only if you finish this potato."

He grabbed the utensil from her hand and held her by the wrists. "No more potatoes unless they have sour cream and chives on them."

"I guess you must be getting well." She smiled and pulled her wrists free.

"I've been well all day. You just didn't notice."

"I noticed that you slept all day—again."

"That's because I was bored watching you read and write and sew. There was nothing else to do." He frowned. He was ready to leave.

"That's the idea," she told him.

"What, to bore me to death? You're holding me here against my will, you know that? I could press charges against you."

Kyla chuckled. "You'll have to think of something better than that. I haven't seen any police around here. Have you?"

Chase watched her gray eyes lighten, her smile made her look happy and relaxed. He knew there was a deeper reason for her commitment to her job other than her wanting the thrill of adventure, but he'd resolved not to try to unearth it until they were back in Kathmandu. He didn't want to ruin the rest of the trip. "I'll wait until we get back to the States then, for a change of venue," he said.

"I didn't know you were going back."

"It would be worth it to see you hauled into court. What you're doing is illegal and unethical, and if you continue I'll be forced to organize a mutiny."

"You think Kibo would turn against me? He loves being here in his village. And you know I'm doing the right thing, deep in your heart." She traced the left side of his chest with her finger.

He didn't move or speak. He was afraid of breaking the spell. He wanted her to keep touching him.

"Tell me," she continued, "what would you have done if I were the one with altitude sickness? Force me out on the trail? Let me keep going? You know there's no cure except rest. And if that doesn't work, there's nothing else to do but to go back down. Am I right?"

She was leaning forward now, with her hands on his shoulders. He felt as if he were smothering in the fragrance from her hair. He knew what he would do if she were sick. He'd hold her in his arms and make her stay in bed for a week. Then he'd have her walk a straight line to check her balance. Fortunately she didn't know about that. He pulled her down until she rested lightly against him.

"You're right," he said, and kissed her cheek.

She lifted herself up and sat next to him. Chase looked at the statue of Buddha, gleaming in the candlelight on the table, smiling his mysterious smile.

"He must know something we don't know," Chase remarked.

Kyla followed his gaze. "He knows everything."

Chase wondered if it was true. Did he know what would happen to them when they got back? If he did, he wasn't telling. He was only smiling.

"Then he knows we're leaving tomorrow," Chase concluded.

Kyla didn't answer, but later in the evening he saw her packing her clothes into the saddlebags, and he knew he had won a small victory. He tried not to think about who would win the next one—the one that really counted.

They started out slowly the next day, taking many breaks for tea and dried fruit. Kyla watched him anxiously, and he smiled reassuringly and walked briskly when she was looking. At one point they seemed to be faced with a solid barrier of high peaks and vertical ice walls, but Kibo pointed out four possible ways of piercing the frontier.

It took them three days, but after they crossed the range they found themselves above the Manang Valley. Even that late in the season, farmers were harvesting a special high-altitude red rice. The trekkers passed women in heavy embroidered dresses carrying baskets of wild herbs. Their brass-and-turquoise earrings hung almost to their shoulders, and their leggings were bunched around their ankles.

Kyla stopped to speak to them and the women pointed to a long narrow valley below, where smoke billowed from a village. There they would find the local shaman, the doctor of traditional medicine, who might assist them in distributing the vitamin A.

Chase took off his pack and leaned over to look down. An entire glacier was visible, from its white cone to the gray trails that forked off into the valley. His heart pounded—not from the altitude this time, but from the excitement of seeing Manang Valley at last.

He told Kyla, "Ask them how long it will take to get down there." He waited impatiently while Kyla translated.

"Three hours, maybe more."

"Let's go."

Kyla shook her head. "It's too late. We'd arrive after dark without a place to stay. We can't just pitch our tents in the middle of town." She studied his face. "I know how eager you are, but you've waited this long, can't you wait until tomorrow?" She put her hand on his shoulder. "The women say the path is steep and slippery and I think the three hours is for them, not us."

"Do you mean we can't go as fast as they can?" He surveyed the women from the baskets on their heads to their straw sandals.

"These women have lived here all their lives," Kyla replied. "They know every crevice, every root along the trail. Also, they say there's a pilgrims' rest house built over the hot springs on our way down."

Chase heard the wistful note in Kyla's voice and saw the look on her face. It was time for a rest. He pictured the rocks, steam and the hot water surrounding them, and argued no more.

They started down the hill and found the rest house. It was old and abandoned, but hot water still bubbled from the springs below and came out through brass waterspouts into a manmade rock pool.

Chase waited in the living room while Kyla took the first bath. Kibo had made a fire in the open fireplace and the delicious smell of red rice cooking filled the air. The anticipation of actually reaching the valley made Chase unable to hold still. He paced in front of the fire, then walked to the door and looked down at the pool. Kyla, wrapped in a towel, was on her way up the steps to the house. Her skin glowed, her eyes sparkled, her hair was twisted on top of her head like Venus's.

"How was it?" His voice sounded gravelly to his ears.

She beamed. "Wonderful."

The rest of the evening passed in slow motion for Chase. First the total immersion in the hot water, draining away all the impatience he had felt that afternoon. Then a pot of rice and herbs and dried apples that they ate together in companionable silence in front of the roaring fire. There was no need to talk. They had said all there was to say.

Before bed he watched Kyla unpin her hair and then she wasn't Venus anymore. She was an earth goddess now, and he couldn't tear his eyes away from her. From his sleeping bag on the other side of the room he watched her sleep. They had almost reached their goal. After that would it all be anticlimax? He had a strange feeling of foreboding.

In the morning fierce winds blew as they climbed a ridge before descending to the village. On the main street, children stopped and stared at them, then ran away only to reappear on roofs or behind windows to peer out at them. By the time they reached the shops and houses, they were followed by a parade of children, who were now brave enough to ask for candy.

Chase and Kyla sat in a restaurant and ordered coffee and warm chapatis.

"Did you see how thin they were?" Chase asked.

"But they couldn't be malnourished," Kyla replied. "They have so much energy."

"The vitamin A deficiency doesn't show up for years, and by the time it does, it's too late. They weren't too shy to ask for candy. Where did they learn that?"

Kyla drew her eyebrows together. "There may have been other trekkers here." She turned around and at the table in the corner saw a bald head rising behind an English-language newspaper. The face finally appeared and Kyla gasped. "Colonel Prajapati."

He raised an eyebrow—not in surprise, but in mild amusement. "We meet again," he said, picking up his coffee cup and joining them at their table. "How fortunate, as I bring you a message from your office in Kathmandu."

"A message? For me?" she asked.

"They gave it to me knowing I was coming this way. Lucky for you that you arrived today, as we're leaving tomorrow." He reached under his wool jacket and pulled out a sealed envelope.

Kyla stared at it. Maybe it was a letter from Lillian. She slit the envelope with her fingernail. The message was brief. More people had signed up for the next trip to China than expected. When would she be back? When would she be free? The words leaped out from the page. China. When?

When? She looked at Chase. He was frowning at the colonel, who spoke as if nothing had happened.

"I must tell you to avoid the sanctuary, if that's where you're headed. There was a flash flood and you can't get past the riverbed. As compensation I've brought my group here to enjoy the hot springs and to look for the elusive yeti."

"The yeti?" Chase and Kyla exchanged an amused look.

"Don't laugh," Colonel Prajapati warned. "Footprints have been seen not far from here."

"Maybe they were mine," Chase suggested, looking down at his boots.

The colonel shrugged. "The yeti has been seen and photographed, you know."

"But not here, not in a village." Kyla set her cup down.

"Ah, no. More's the pity. This is the only place within a hundred miles to get a decent cup of coffee. But we take day hikes up into the gorge, cameras ever ready. We're always back for dinner, though. There's nothing like a home-cooked meal after stalking the yeti all day. I can recommend the barbecued goat at the Ghyaru up the street."

"Right now we're looking for the shaman," Kyla said.

The colonel nodded. "I can show you where he resides, but I can tell you a shaman is nothing more than a witch doctor. His idea of treatment is to appease the evil spirits. I trust you have no problem with evil spirits, Doctor?"

"None at all," Chase assured him, annoyed at the colonel for sitting at their table and spoiling their breakfast with his long-winded comments.

After Colonel Prajapati had finished his coffee, he motioned for Kyla and Chase to follow him. He led them back up the street, then down a narrow alley to a wooden door with the shaman's name carved on it in Sanskrit.

"Until this evening, then," the colonel called over his shoulder with a smile.

"Not if I can help it," Chase muttered under his breath.

They found the shaman on the second floor, in a cubicle behind the crowded waiting room. Long hair framed his thin, ascetic-looking face, and he wore a clean white robe. He shook Chase's hand and looked into his eyes, perhaps trying to determine whether Chase was worthy of his attention. Then he asked Chase if he had any new ulcer medicine, since he himself was suffering from one.

When the shaman went out to get some herbs to share with him, Chase emptied his backpack to find something appropriate. Kyla looked around the small area.

"What could cause the man to have an ulcer here, of all places? Where's the stress and the strain?"

Chase held up a bottle of pills and shrugged. "You never know. Maybe the villagers expect miracles from the doctor. They do at home, and that can put a lot of stress on a man. High expectations, a low incidence of miracles—it all adds up."

Kyla laced her fingers together. "When are you going to tell him about the vitamins for the children?"

Chase smiled. "We're exchanging information first. Professional courtesy. He's going to show me how he treats local problems without Western medicine. We might have a miniconference right here. Why don't you go find us someplace to stay? Anywhere but where the colonel is. I'll meet you in the restaurant."

She paused in the doorway, strangely reluctant to leave him. They had been together every minute of every day and night; and now he wanted her to leave, to break the bond between them, and it filled her with sadness. An irrational, ridiculous feeling for someone who'd spent all of her adult life alone—in a crowd, but alone all the same.

She straightened her shoulders, said goodbye and marched up the street where she saw Kibo engaged in lively conversation with one of the colonel's guides. He hurried over to her and told her the other group was lodged at the only hotel. Fortunately, he, Kibo, happened to have a cousin who was willing to put them in her extra bedroom.

Kyla followed the Sherpa down a maze of tiny alleys until he paused in front of a door that squeaked on leather hinges when he pushed it open. The round-faced woman who greeted them smiled broadly. Her smooth hair was parted in the middle and her homespun wool dress grazed the tops of her boots. The smell of incense permeated the hallway, which led to the guest room. Kyla stared in dismay at the double bed in the center of the large sunlit room.

How would she explain her choice of quarters to Chase? He might assume she couldn't resist him anymore. How could she sleep next to him and not give in to the passion she felt every time he looked at her or said her name? She murmured a few words in Nepali, assured Kibo she was well pleased with his cousin's house and her spare room, and hurried back to meet Chase.

He was pacing up and down in front of the restaurant, and her heart skipped a beat as if she hadn't seen him for weeks.

"The man is amazing," he told her. "There's a lot we could learn from him. But right now, we're going to start handing out the vitamins. Can you believe we're here? I can't believe we're here." He grinned at her and took her hand. His excitement was contagious. It flowed from his body to hers and she knew she would not have missed this moment for anything.

By afternoon the shaman and the local mayor had every child under twelve lined up outside the entrance to the civil government office. There were girls wearing long gold earrings with babies on their backs and boys with bright red cheeks in short pants. A small child in her mother's arms would not stop crying until Chase took a vitamin pill from behind her ear. The she laughed and swallowed it. By the end of the day there was a crowd of children who had received their vitamins but who stayed around to watch the fun.

Chase and Kyla were the best show in town, at least until the colonel found a yeti. Even as they packed up their supplies, children still hung around, leaning against the building, waiting to follow them home. Chase scooped up the small girl who'd cried earlier, and held her against his chest. She buried her face in Chase's shoulder and Kyla saw the look in his eyes.

She knew how it felt to carry a child in her arms. She knew the longing to have one of her own to cherish and to watch grow. She turned away, unable to watch anymore as Chase swung the child by the arms to the ground. They walked down the back alleys in silence, with the wind sweeping down from the glacier and the sound of chimes in the air.

The smell of incense greeted them when they opened the door to Kibo's cousin's house and tiptoed down the hall to avoid disturbing the family at dinner. A gas lamp on the wall illuminated the bed; its covers were turned back to reveal linen sheets, clean but yellowed with age. After so many nights in a sleeping bag, Kyla had an overwhelming urge to take off her heavy clothes instantly and crawl between the sheets.

She was prepared for a reaction from Chase, but his disarming smile caught her off guard. Did he have the same overwhelming urge? She fingered the heavy embroidered bedspread and stood at the foot of the bed. "The hotel was full," she said to break the silence. "I was lucky to find this."

He nodded solemnly. "It reminds me of the Himalayan View Hotel."

"There's no view here."

"I was thinking more of the sleeping arrangements."

"I couldn't help that," she explained quickly. "If I could have found another room..."

He put his hand on her hair and tucked a windblown strand behind her ear. "It wouldn't have been the same." His hand smoothed her tousled curls and his fingers moved to the back of her neck.

"What are you going to do tomorrow?" she asked, pulling away to wash her hands in the basin on the stand next to the bed.

Chase watched her dry her hands. "There are little villages scattered all over the valley. The shaman is going with us to help out." He paused. "You're coming, aren't you?" He leaned against the bed, suddenly too tired to stand, too scared to speak. He'd just realized she had said, "What are *you* doing tomorrow," instead of *we*.

"Do you need me?" Her voice was casual, but he wasn't fooled.

"Yes, I need you." He pulled her down to sit next to him on the bed. "Not to hand out pills, I can do that. I need you to tell me, right now just what drives you to go on your trips." He'd promised himself he wouldn't question her, but his hunger to know the truth was suddenly overwhelming.

Her face half in shadow, she looked over his shoulder, refusing to meet his gaze. He wanted to shake her, demand an honest answer.

"What I need to do," she said carefully, "is to do something different for a while."

"For a while?" He exploded. "How long is that?"

She stood and walked to the window. "I don't know, but I know that I want to be alone. I have to think things over." Her face was pinched and tight, her brow lined with worry. "I had things all figured out before I met you, before we came on this trip. Now I'm mixed up."

"Mixed up about me?" he asked.

She shook her head. "Mixed up about myself. About what I want. About what I can have. I had come to terms with my limitations before, but now you've made me want things I can't have."

"You *can* have them," he insisted.

"No, I can't." She turned her back to him and stared out into the darkness. "I told you my mother died when I was twenty. I didn't tell you that she died of Huntington's disease."

Chase felt his chest contract. It explained everything. She had inherited the disease from her mother and her days were numbered. He didn't care. He wanted to share those days with her, every precious one of them.

"When did you find out? When did you take the test?"

"I didn't take it. I'm not going to take it." She turned and stared at him, gray eyes defiant.

He felt like laughing and crying at the same time. She might not have it. She couldn't have it. It wouldn't be fair. "Why don't you take the test?" he asked softly.

"I don't want to know. I thought it was obvious." She walked back to the bed and sat next to him. "I heard about the test when they discovered the gene marker. I was driving across the Golden Gate Bridge on my way to my father's house. I had to pull off at the toll plaza because I was crying so hard I couldn't see." She clenched her fists. "But I've never cried about it again. Don't you understand?"

She leaned forward and held him with the intensity of her gaze.

"I have a happy life. Surely you can see that. How much happier would I be if I found I didn't have Huntington's?" She paused and then answered her own question. "A little, maybe. But not that much. But what if I found I was carrying the gene for Huntington's, like my mother?" Her eyes were wide now and Chase heard the pain in her voice, saw it in her face and felt it in the core of his body.

"How much more miserable would I be?" She got up and stood at the foot of the bed. "A whole lot."

Her voice was steady, but he could see she was trembling and he reached for her and pulled her onto his lap. Her arms crept around his neck and she hid her face in his shoulder, but he felt no tears.

"I understand that," he said soothingly. "You do have a wonderful life, full of thrills and excitement, but I... I—" He broke off, his throat closing. Did his love for her give him the right to interfere in her life? To persuade her to make a decision that could cause her misery for the rest of her life?

"I love you," he whispered and she tightened her arms around him. "And I want to spend the rest of my life with you. If you don't want to take the test, it's all right with me."

He felt her body stiffen and she sat up straight in his lap and shook her head. "But I've already told you. I'm not spending the rest of my life with anybody. You of all people should understand that Huntington's is one of those diseases that's harder on the family than the patient. That's why I live alone. That's why I'm going to continue to live alone, and why I'm not going to have a family."

He put his arms around her waist and looked into her eyes, which were dark with the frustration of having to put up with his stubborn persistence. "All right, I won't be your family. But I'll be a part of you and you'll be a part of me."

"No!" It was more than a word, it was a cry of anguish. "I don't have lovers. I didn't tell you the real reason before, but now you know. You know everything about me, but you still don't understand." She stood and clenched her fists, her arms hanging stiffly at her sides.

"I might understand if I thought you didn't love me. But I think you do."

She stood in front of him in her pale blue sweater and black stretch pants. "Yes. I didn't plan that. I don't know when it happened or how. But we were not meant to be, you and I. Deep down you know that, don't you?" She was begging him to understand, but he shook his head.

"I don't know that and you don't know that." He stood. "And we won't know the answer unless you take the test."

She winced as if he'd touched her with a hot poker, and he held her by the arms. "I'm selfish," he admitted. "I want you to take the test because it's the only way I have a chance with you. If you don't have it, we get married and live happily ever after. If you have it, we'll at least have some time together. And when you get sick and you need someone, I'll be there. Instead of strangers to take care of you, you'll have me. I want to spend every day with you and every night, from now on, for the rest of our lives, no matter what happens."

Her eyes never left his face, and he thought for a moment he might have broken through her defenses. But when he finished speaking, she shook her head slowly.

"What about children?" she asked. "I know how much you love them. I can see it in your eyes and hear it when you talk about the children of the Manang Valley. Do you know how it feels to grow up knowing your mother has an incurable disease? If you did, you'd know it's out of the question. I can't even consider it. I never could."

"But if you did take the test..."

"No."

"Then don't take it. I don't need children. I'll have the children of the Manang Valley and the Amazon Basin and wherever else in the world they need me. I don't have to have my own children. But I do have to have you." His throat hurt, his eyes stung, but he hadn't changed her mind. If anything he had made her more determined to hold her ground. He threw up his arms.

"I see you've made your decision. It's the right one for you. Keep leading tours, go wherever you want. I'll come if I can. If I can't, I'll work and wait for you. It doesn't matter. As long as you come back to me, come home to me." There was a lump in his throat so large that he couldn't say another word. But he had her attention.

"I can't do that to you—be half a wife, with no children and no time together. You deserve more than that, and I can't give you more than that. It sounds great. I'm off in China, sometimes you get a postcard from me, saying 'Having a wonderful time.' But would I even be able to have a wonderful time knowing you were back in your operating room with a lobby full of patients and no one to help you?

"That's what I don't know. And what's worse—" she sat on the bed and turned her back to him "—what's worse is that I don't know if I can live without knowing if I have the gene for Huntington's." Her shoulders shook with sobs and he held her against his chest, feeling her tears fall on his fingers.

When she stopped crying she gave him a watery smile, then washed her face and changed her sweater. "I'm hungry," she said. "Let's go to the hotel to eat. I have to speak to the colonel."

The muscles in his chest tightened. "What about?"

"I'm going to ask him if I can tag along on the trip back."

He nodded slowly, trying to understand, trying to accept the inevitable. He knew she would find a way to get away from him, and there was no way to stop her if she was determined to go.

"You want more time here anyway," she continued. "You and the shaman can trade secrets. Kibo will bring you back when you're ready." Her voice was so matter-of-fact she might have been talking about a walk to the corner store instead of a trek across a major mountain range. His mind reeling, he fought for control of his emotions.

"Where will you be?" he asked.

"They still want me in China. That's what the letter said," she answered. Then, without waiting to see if he had something to add, she strode to the door and stepped out. Chase had to move quickly to catch up.

They walked to the hotel without speaking. Chase felt his insides being ripped to shreds. He was a man of action, of quick decisions in life-and-death matters. But he was helpless to change what was happening in his own life.

They ate in the dining room. Chase had no idea what the meal consisted of, but he knew someone was playing a Himalayan lute and the sound mingled with the wind from the mountains. Kyla's eyes were unnaturally bright—from tears or excitement, he didn't know which. Her cheeks were pink and he stared at her, trying to memorize her face, knowing he might never see her again, and not knowing what he could do about it.

He waited in the small lobby after dinner while she went upstairs to see the colonel, to ask if she could go back with him. When she came down the narrow stairway he knew the answer.

"What time are you leaving?" he asked with stiff lips.

"Early. As soon as the café opens. We'll meet there. Don't come to see me off, please." There was a catch in her voice that made his chest hurt. He had never read about heartbreak in any medical journal, but he knew now how it felt; and he knew there was no cure.

As they walked the narrow streets for the last time, Chase spoke. "You told me once that the people on your treks only remember the good parts."

She looked up at him. "Will you?"

He shrugged; the pain was too deep to bear. "Sure. No problem, because it's been all good parts. If you ever need a recommendation..."

"Thanks," she said with a forced smile. "I'll remember that."

Those were the last words she spoke to him that night. They trudged back to the small stone house, Chase's feet feeling as heavy as if he'd just scaled Annapurna, and his heart like a stone in his chest.

He made no pretense of sleeping. Kyla turned her back to him once again, just as she had turned her back on his proposals. He couldn't believe it was their last night together, but if it was, he didn't want to spend it this way. When he couldn't stand the tension any longer, he reached for her and pulled her to him. A ragged sigh escaped her lips and she relaxed against his body. He didn't know what to say; he'd said it all. He felt her heart beating in time to his and he held her until dawn.

She dressed quickly and stood at the door, hesitating for only a moment. She raised her hand and waved.

He leaned against the wall, his arms crossed. ''Send me a card from China.''

She nodded. ''Having a wonderful time. Wish you were here.'' Then she turned and was gone. Gone out of his life.

Chapter Ten

The trip back to Kathmandu passed in a blur for Kyla. She put one foot ahead of the other. She pretended interest in finding the yeti. She ate fish from the Kali Gandaki River and passed through oak and rhododendron forests. She took pictures of small children and old men in tribal costumes. She traded gossip with Colonel Prajapati and told stories around the dinner table at night.

No one knew that the real Kyla was not there at all. The woman who did all those things was a robot, a hollow shell with nothing inside. Her heart and soul remained in the Manang Valley with Chase. Her thoughts traveled back to the small village she had come from, just as her feet traveled forward toward Kathmandu.

She didn't try to make excuses for herself. There were none. She didn't try to rationalize her behavior during the past several weeks; she couldn't. She was only capable of doing what she had to do, what she had trained herself to do: think ahead—of the next trip, of the next group. Don't look back.

When they arrived in the crowded bustling city Kyla went to the local office of Adventure Travel. Overjoyed to see her, they handed her an itinerary that had her leaving in two days. She had no need to return to the States or meet the group ahead of time. They would proceed to Beijing. Kyla stared at the list of arrival-and-departure times and places.

Then suddenly she looked up. "I can't go."

"Can't go?" The director looked at her over his wire-rimmed glasses. "It's the trip of a lifetime." His gaze traveled over her wrinkled shirt, her boots still caked with dirt and her hair in its usual tangle. Her gray eyes were wide and clear, with a distant, faraway look in them.

"What happened out there? You look funny."

Kyla rubbed her cheek and looked out the window. "I feel funny. I have to go to California before I do anything else. To take care of some family business. Then I'll be back." She drew her eyebrows together. "I'm sorry I'm letting you down."

He shrugged. "Let us know what happens. Keep in touch."

Kyla nodded absentmindedly.

On the plane to San Francisco, Kyla told herself she was doing this for herself and not for Chase. But she could no longer distinguish where one left off and the other began. She only knew that she had to take the test. She could no longer live her life under a cloud of uncertainty. If the test was positive for the Huntington's gene, then she would continue to explore the world as she'd been doing, knowing it was the right thing to do until she was unable to function any longer.

But if she found she didn't have it, she would have other options. She loosened her seat belt, then pressed her head against the window and gave in to her fantasies. She imagined walking into Chase's hospital to tell him the good news. She remembered how he'd looked, the first day she'd ever seen him, his dark eyes staring at her from above his surgeon's mask. She thought of him standing in the rain the day Mr. Wangchen gave them the carpet, the day she touched the prayer wheel at the temple and looked at the erotic carvings.

When she arrived in San Francisco, she found it cold and modern. She checked into a small hotel near Fisherman's Wharf and walked up and down the streets seeing clean high-rise apartment buildings. She signed up for the test and filled out reams of forms, all in triplicate. For whom to notify in case of emergency she listed her aunt and her father and Chase. She took the test and then settled down to wait for the results.

She was alone in the cool city by the bay, and that was the way she wanted it. She called no one, told no one she was there. Weeks went by while she waited for the results. Rain blew in off the ocean and drenched the streets. The tourists went home and Kyla felt she had San Francisco to herself.

Most days she put on her hiking boots and walked from one end of the city to the other. At the end of the day she was too tired to think, and that was good. Finally there was only one week before she would learn the results. And then there was only one weekend.

For Chase, life returned to normal very quickly after he got back to his clinic. He thought he had worked hard before he left, but he was working twice as hard now. He'd always put in long days; now he seldom even went home.

He slept on a cot in his office at the hospital and went right back to work in the morning. When he did go home to his small apartment he saw the carpet hanging on his wall, the one that was only half his.

He tried to imagine Kyla rafting down the Yangtze River, her hair ruffled by the wind, her group watching her, hanging on her every word, and he was consumed with a longing so intense it made him ache all over. One Sunday he drove to the airport and stood in the lounge looking up at the list of departures. There was a plane leaving for Beijing at two and he almost bought a ticket. Then he realized that he wouldn't know where to find her on the Yangtze River, or even where the Yangtze River was. Even if he did know, she wouldn't want to see him. He turned around and walked out.

Maybe he'd write her a letter, something casual, with news of some of the patients she'd remember. There had to be a way of getting mail to her, even on the Yangtze River. The next day he took a taxi to the Adventure Travel office.

He stood in front of a cluttered desk and asked for Kyla Tanner's forwarding address. The receptionist thumbed through her file and looked up at him.

"Vista del Mar Hotel, Fisherman's Wharf, San Francisco. We had a card from her last week. Shall I write it down for you?"

Chase rocked back on his heels. "No. I think I can remember it. But I thought she was in China. Is she already back?"

The woman shook her head. "She decided not to go. She had some family business in San Francisco. Then she'll be back."

Chase went out the door and walked up the street in a fog of disbelief. Why didn't she tell him?

* * *

It took him a few days to line up another doctor to cover for him. He tried to stop asking himself why she hadn't told him. Then he was back at the airport, this time buying a ticket for San Francisco and getting on the plane.

After they landed through layers of cool gray fog, Chase rented a car and drove to Kyla's hotel. It was Friday evening in San Francisco, but Saturday morning in Kathmandu, and Chase hadn't slept for twenty-four hours.

The hotel clerk told him that Kyla was out, so Chase reserved the room next to hers. Then he paced back and forth in the lobby, waiting for her to come back.

He paused at the double glass doors and looked out at the rain-washed street. Where could she be on a rainy Friday evening? Who would she be with? What would she say when she saw him? His jet-lagged mind began to play tricks on him and he saw her a dozen times in the street. Every woman in a raincoat was her. Every time the telephone rang in the lobby he imagined she was calling him.

He finally collapsed into a large soft chair facing the entrance. As soon as he sat down, she walked through the door. She wasn't wearing a raincoat. She was wearing a bright red jacket and black pants that were tucked into her boots. Walking across a lobby or down a narrow footpath in the Himalayas, she had the same spring in her step. He tried to call her name, to stride over to her and grab her by the arm, but he couldn't move or speak.

Finally he forced himself to stand. The hotel clerk said something to her in a low voice and she turned around. Their eyes met and her room key clattered to the floor. Her face was suddenly drained of all color and, afraid she was going to faint, he rushed forward to hold her.

"How did you know?" Her voice—still husky, still beautiful—faltered.

"I went over to Adventure Travel. They gave me your address."

"Oh."

"You came to take the test, didn't you? Why didn't you tell me?"

"Chase, this is something I had to do alone. Monday I'll know the results. I was going to tell you then, if—"

"If it was negative." He finished her sentence for her.

She nodded.

"And if it's positive?"

"I'll go back to work," she answered briskly, recovering her composure. "As if it never happened."

"What about me?" He picked up her key and guided her toward the elevator.

Her lips trembled. "You shouldn't have come."

"But now that I'm here—" he pushed the button for the tenth floor "—what are you going to do about me?"

She shook her head helplessly and they rode up in silence. Their feet sank into the thick hall carpeting as they walked to her room. Chase unlocked her door, and she looked up at him inquiringly.

He smiled. "I need to be fed and entertained. It's not often I come back for the weekend. I suppose you've already seen and done everything without me."

She ran her finger along the edge of the door, a half smile tugging at the corner of her mouth. "I haven't done anything but walk from one end of the city to the other."

He touched her hair. "In the rain," he said.

"In the rain, in the sun, in the wind and in the fog. It doesn't matter."

"It matters now. We're going to do the town, and we're going to start in half an hour. Did you bring a dress?" His gaze traveled over the curves outlined by her shirt and her form-fitting pants. She looked stunned, first at his being there, then at his rapid-fire orders. She nodded.

"Good, then get into it. I'll be next door." He opened the connecting door between their rooms and then closed it behind him.

Kyla stood in the middle of the room staring out the window without seeing the lights of the city below. Chase was in San Francisco, here in this hotel, in the next room. Mechanically she walked to the bathroom, turned on the hot water and filled the tub. He had come halfway around the world to spend the weekend with her and it threw her into turmoil. Ever since the first time she'd seen him he had the ability to shake up her world and turn it upside down.

She started when she head a knock on the connecting door and his voice calling out her name. "I'm in the tub," she answered.

"Come on out." His voice sounded close by. He was in her room, on the other side of the bathroom door. "I've got to have something to eat."

She stepped out of the tub and wrapped herself in a large towel, then opened the door a crack. "How about a nice baked potato?" she suggested.

At that, he came through and took her by the shoulders. "I told you never to mention potatoes to me again," he growled. Then he kissed her fiercely.

She grabbed the top of the towel with one hand and wrapped her other arm around his neck. "Be careful, you'll get your suit wet." Her heart pounding, she stepped back. "I've never seen you in a suit before." The lines around his eyes had deepened. He looked tired and worried. It was up to her to erase those lines, to make him forget why he had come, to make him have a good time. It might be their last weekend together.

"Just give me a few minutes to get dressed," she said, pushing him out of the doorway. Chase was back in her life and she felt hope stirring deep within her. But along with hope came despair. How could she ever say goodbye to him again?

He waited for her in the corridor and when she opened the door he smiled. "I remember that blouse. You wore it to dinner with me once." His eyes traveled the length of her handwoven skirt and came back to the pale pink silk blouse. He leaned forward and kissed her hair, then her forehead and lips. Her knees shook, and she didn't know if she'd be able to step down the hallway to the elevator. Somehow she made it out to the sidewalk, where Chase hailed a taxi.

She was reminded of that other night, so long ago, in front of a hotel in Kathmandu. Again Chase directed the driver to take them out of the city, this time to Sausalito, to a hotel dining room built into a steep cliff overlooking the bay.

At the restaurant they ordered and Kyla leaned back in her chair. "You confused me that night we went to the Vasera Hotel. You never said you were taking me to dinner."

"You mean you ate before I came?"

"No. I was too nervous. I didn't know what you wanted." She traced the rim of her wineglass with her finger. "What *did* you want?"

He touched her hand. "To see you. To talk to you. To tell you about the Manang Valley."

"You could have done that at the hospital."

"Yes, but then I wouldn't have seen you in your pink silk blouse, which matches the color of your cheeks when you're excited or embarrassed."

She felt herself blush now, and looked down. "How was your trip back? Did Kibo take good care of you?"

He nodded. "We didn't take the suspension bridge. I made him go around. It took longer, but I couldn't face it without you."

"I'm sorry."

"Don't be. It saved me from making a fool of myself again."

"It takes courage to admit you're afraid." The words died in Kyla's throat. She gazed at the lights in the harbor across the bay. There was a long pause.

"Yes, it does, doesn't it?" he replied.

She looked at him, her eyes bright with tears. "I'm scared to death, Chase."

He covered her hand with his. His voice deepened. "I know you are."

The waiter brought their soup and Kyla brushed her eyes with her napkin and cleared her throat. Chase's eyes were suspiciously red around the rims.

"I promised myself I'd show you a good time this weekend. I'm off to a good start, aren't I?" Kyla asked with a smile.

"No more tears," he said. "That's an order."

She swallowed hard, then held up two fingers in a Scout's salute. "I promise." She concentrated on her soup, and when she finished she looked up at Chase. "What do you want to do this weekend? How am I supposed to entertain you?"

He smiled a slow, lazy smile that made her heart pump wildly. How had she forgotten the way his mouth curved?

"Well..." He hesitated and gazed at her face, savoring the sight of her as if she were a clear pool in the middle of the desert. He crossed his arms as the waiter served their entrées. "Let's go to Angel Island and Alcatraz and the Exploratorium and Fort Point and—"

She laughed. "We only have a weekend."

"We could have the rest of our lives."

"Chase," she warned. "No tears and no could haves or should haves."

He held out his hand. "It's a deal. Tell me about your trip back with the colonel. Did you ever see the yeti?"

She shook her head. "Not even a footprint."

"Did you camp by streams, look up at the mountains, talk to villagers, take part in local festivals?"

"That's *my* philosophy, but it's not the colonel's. We marched eighteen miles a day. Tea at ten and rest stop at four. Tents up and bedtime at nine-thirty."

"I wouldn't have liked that. I'm glad I hired you instead of him. And I'm glad you didn't miss me."

She watched his hands—the fingers that restored sight and soothed the tired and sick. "I didn't have time to miss you." *But if we're separated again, I don't know how I'll stand it,* she added silently.

They ate the rest of their meal in silence. After Chase had paid the check, she stood and let him put her sweater over her shoulders.

"Let's go. I want to ride the cable car back to the hotel," he said.

They took a cab to Powell Street. Because of the light rain, no one was waiting for the next antique red-and-gold car. When it arrived, Chase sat on the outside bench and Kyla stood on the running board. As it began its roller-coaster ride down Hyde Street toward the bay, she leaned against Chase; he put his arms around her and held her tightly as if he'd never let her go.

Then she swung onto the seat next to him and he kissed her hungrily. They were both oblivious to the conductor and the grip man who called out the names of the streets. Kyla didn't hear the sound of the bells or see the lights reflected in the waters of the bay. She was lost in the magic of the kiss she'd remembered and yearned for; the kiss she'd thought she'd never experience again.

The conductor smiled benevolently. "End of the line," he called.

They stepped off and Chase put his arm around her shoulders and yawned.

"How long since you've had some sleep?" she asked as they walked slowly back to the hotel.

"Can't remember. Maybe on the plane."

"You have to go to bed soon, or we'll never make it to Angel Island and the Exploratorium and all that."

He smiled and agreed to everything she said. They said good-night in the hall in front of their respective doors. Chase leaned down and kissed her lightly on the lips. "Will you wake me in the morning?"

"What time?" She rested her cheek against his, to feel the roughness, to make sure she wasn't dreaming.

"Whenever you wake up. I'll tell you to go away, that it's the middle of the night, but do it anyway."

"It won't be too early," she promised. "You need to make up for lost sleep."

He nuzzled her chin and kissed the back of her ear. "I lost some sleep, but I found you." He tightened his arms around her. "I thought I'd lost you and I'd never see you again. I don't ever want to let you go." His voice was loaded with the emotions held in check for so long.

She kissed him and slipped out of his arms, blindly reaching for her doorknob and letting herself into her room. After she had changed into her nightgown she paced back and forth from the window to the bed.

Two more days. Seeing him again, spending every minute of every day together was going to make it so much harder to say goodbye forever. But she didn't have the strength to tell him to go away now, to leave her to face the test results by herself. She was too weak. Just as she threw herself across the bed, there was a knock on the connecting door.

She jumped up and opened it. Chase stood with his shirt unbuttoned, his hair hanging across his forehead. He reached for the switch and turned off the light. The pale moon that came from behind a rain cloud turned the room to silver.

"Why aren't you asleep?" His voice was drowsy and made her tremble with a desire so strong she couldn't speak.

"Who are you? Colonel Prajapati?" she asked finally, struggling to keep her voice steady. "I didn't know we had a lights-out policy."

He flashed her a grin. "This is *my* tour, and the only policy we have is to do what feels good. Get into bed. Did I ever tell you that all interns in family medicine are required to learn massage therapy?"

She lay facedown on the cool sheets. "I don't think you did," she mumbled into the pillow. His hands were on her shoulders, sending shudders of pleasure across her back and down her spine. He kneaded the muscles in her neck, then trailed his hands down to the curve of her hips.

"That feels so good," she murmured. All the tension was gone. She was putty in his hands. At that moment she belonged to him. She would have done anything he asked. But he didn't say anything. He let his hands do the talking. And then she was asleep—a deep dreamless sleep that soothed her tattered nerves and restored her equilibrium.

Chase sat on the edge of her bed watching her shoulders move in time to her breathing. He'd been afraid she'd be too tense to sleep. He didn't like the smudges under her eyes. She looked as if she needed rest more than he did. He wanted to lie down next to her, to hold her, to erase the sadness of that last night in the Manang Valley. He wanted to make this the first night of the rest of their lives together.

But he stood carefully and went back to his room. Even though it was three in the afternoon, Kathmandu time, he fell asleep.

The next thing he knew the sun was shining into his room and Kyla was sitting on the edge of his bed wearing a red sweater and blue jeans. She smelled like soap and cotton and fresh air. He reached for her and pulled her down on top of him. She tasted like coffee and toothpaste and her own brand of sunshine. She kissed him with so much enthusiasm that he was about to suggest scrapping all plans for exploring the city to spend the day in bed.

He propped himself up against the headboard and cupped her face in his hands. "Is this the usual wakeup call or have I died and gone to heaven?"

"This is what you ordered, Doctor." She smiled and fireworks went off in his head. If he could have her for the rest of his life, would every day be the Fourth of July? He studied her face. The dark circles were gone from under her eyes. With his thumb he traced the outline of her lips, so sweetly familiar and so desirable, he felt the passion rise inside him. He would never let her go again. Never.

Chase stood and staggered toward the bathroom. "I'm going to take a shower. Save some coffee for me."

Kyla nodded. "Let's go to Angel Island today and rent bicycles."

"Okay," he called above the sound of the running water. He felt like singing and shouting with joy. She looked so good, so happy, so carefree, that he couldn't believe the test result would be positive. And if it was, she would have to accept the fact that he was going to be part of her life from now on.

After his shower and a quick breakfast, they took a cab to Pier 54 and boarded the ferry. The wind was whipping up a froth on the bay, and the sun was shining on the green hills of Marin County. Chase put up the hood of Kyla's jacket and pulled the drawstrings tight. Then he turned her around to face the Bay Bridge and the hills of the East Bay.

"That's where I grew up," he said.

She took his hands from around her waist and held them tightly. "Do your parents know you're here?"

He rested his chin on her head. "No."

"Are you going to see them?"

"I have a pretty full schedule," he replied. "Besides..." His voice trailed off.

"You wouldn't know what to tell them—" she completed his sentence "—or how to explain what you're doing here."

He ignored her last remark. He was trying not to think about the purpose of this trip. He was trying to pretend there was no Monday. "Would you like to meet them?"

"I wouldn't know what to say."

"Don't worry about that. They'd make it easy for you. 'What do you think of Piedmont? Or would you prefer to live in Hillsborough? Do you like brick or flagstone on the patio? Golf at the country club or tennis? Since doctors work long hours when they're starting out, you'll want to join the Junior League and the Daughters of the Golden West.'"

Kyla smiled.

"Do you get the picture? They'd *love* to meet you. They *want* me to get married."

"And have children," she added.

He tightened his arms around her. "That's up to me," he said between clenched teeth. "I think we've already had this conversation." He turned her around to face him. Her hair escaped from her hood and blew across her face. She stared straight ahead. "I thought we weren't going to spoil the weekend by talking about the future, but if you insist . . ." He led her to a deck chair and sat down next to her. "You haven't told me why you changed your mind, why you took the test after all."

She folded her arms on her lap and looked past him at the waves. "You helped me make the decision by telling me what you thought. But I haven't changed my mind about the results. My life will go on as planned after Monday, just the way it has."

He stared at her, numb with disbelief. "I'm supposed to let you go on Monday, no matter what the results are?"

She pressed her lips together. "You'll have to."

"Why, because I'll interfere with your fun-packed schedule? Because you think I'll stop you from having another great adventure?"

She shook her head.

"Then what's the problem?"

She shifted her gaze to his face. "The problem is that you're a doctor, not a tourist or a tour guide. You might enjoy another hike or two, but what about medicine? You've spent years training to do what you do, and you're not prepared to chuck it all to follow me around the world. Come on, Chase, isn't that the truth?"

"You're right. I do want to practice medicine."

The ferry whistle blew, announcing their arrival at Angel Island, and Kyla put her hands over her ears. Chase thought it was to block out his words as well as the sound of the loud whistle. She was under stress and she couldn't think straight. He shouldn't have said anything. He was adding to her stress, instead of making her feel better.

He led her ashore where they rented bikes and pedaled up and down the hills of the island. They caught spectacular glimpses of San Francisco outlined against the blue sky, and paid a nostalgic visit to the old fort.

Kyla felt her cheeks stinging from exertion and windburn. The muscles in her thighs ached and she didn't protest when they got on the next ferry for San Francisco. Chase pulled her onto his lap on the same deck chair she'd sat in on the way over. This trip, they were the only ones on the deck.

"Are you having a good time?" he asked, his lips next to her ear.

"Mmm-hmm," she said, sighing with contentment. "Was it worth the plane ride? Seven thousand miles for a good bed in a nice hotel and a decent cup of coffee?"

"That's not what I came for." His hand moved up under her sweater, feeling warm against her skin.

She shivered with pleasure and buried her face in his shoulder. "It isn't?"

"No." He kissed her neck, then trailed his lips to the hollow in her throat. "I came for some cracked crab and sourdough bread." His hands were under her breasts now.

She sighed once more and gave in to the sensations that made her forget the boat rocking gently beneath her, the cries of the gulls overhead and the creaking of the wooden deck. She didn't pull away until the whistle blew, announcing their arrival back at Pier 54.

On the way to the hotel they stopped to buy a whole cooked Dungeness crab and a loaf of crusty French bread and a bottle of wine. They ate in Chase's room at the table by the window.

After dinner it was Kyla's turn to give Chase a back rub. She felt the planes of his broad back under her palms and heard him moan with pleasure until he told her to stop.

"I'm only human," he said, his voice thick with desire.

She stood and stared down at the lower half of his body, covered with only a sheet, and felt a wave of passion hit her. All she had to do was to pull that sheet back and crawl into his bed next to him and feel his arms around her. It would be a night to remember. Then if she said goodbye to him on Monday, she would at least have the memory of this one night of love.

Yes, he was only human, and so was she. Human enough to want what she couldn't have—Chase. She lifted the sheet and pulled it up around his shoulders.

He turned over and crossed his arms under his head. His eyes were half open, making him almost irresistible. He gave her a slow smile. "Aren't you going to say good-night?"

"Good night."

"Not like that." He held out his arms and without hesitation she went into them. He embraced her so tightly she felt the heat of his body through her sweater. Their lips met and the pounding of her heart drowned out all the reasons why she couldn't do this just once. But when she started to pull her sweater off over her head, a warning bell went off somewhere deep within her. She sat up slowly and straightened her clothes.

Chase's eyes darkened. He ran his hand through his hair. "Even though we're down at sea level, I see the rules are still in effect."

"I'm sorry." She backed her way to the connecting door, knees shaking, hands trembling.

He didn't answer. Kyla went into her own room, wondering how she would find the strength to get through one more day. How would she find the willpower to say good-bye? She lay in her bed listening to the dim sounds of the city. The clang of the cable cars reminded her of the wind in her hair and Chase's lips on hers. He had come seven thousand miles to be with her.

They had walked over mountains, crossed rivers, shared the ups and downs of a rugged trip. Her life was happy, but how much happier would it be if she could share it with Chase? One hundred times? No. Much more. Chase was not an ordinary man. It was not chance that had brought her to his hospital. It was fate. The gods had sent her there, and who was she to turn down a gift from the gods? What right did she have to turn her back on him?

She jumped out of bed and knocked on the connecting door. Before he could answer she was back at his bedside.

He blinked and rubbed his eyes. He reached for her and pulled her down on top of him. "Is this a dream?"

She swallowed hard. "If you still want me, I mean if the test is positive and you still want me, I . . . I . . ." The tears ran down her face and she brushed them away impatiently.

"I want you," he said, his voice unsteady. "I wasn't going to let you go. I was going to kidnap you if necessary. It will be easier this way—your coming voluntarily." He grinned at her. "Now, go back to bed. We have a full day tomorrow."

She nodded and flew across the room. She would never be alone again. Somehow, somewhere, they would be together, for richer or poorer, in sickness and in health. But she would not think about that part. Not now.

Chapter Eleven

The next day passed in a blur. Chase kept her so busy she didn't have time to think. From brunch at an elegant restaurant to feeding the ducks at a pond on a museum's grounds, then a tour of the Exploratorium where they crawled through the tactile dome. Then dinner in the Mission at a mom-and-pop restaurant and another cable-car ride, until Kyla fell into bed exhausted.

Kyla packed her suitcase in the early-morning light on Monday. She wanted to be ready to leave, no matter what news she heard. She wanted to get on with her life—hers and Chase's. Her hands shook as she crammed her sweaters and hiking boots into her bag and latched it. For the first time, she wished Chase had never come. She dreaded seeing the look on his face if the answer was positive. It would be easier to take the bad news by herself.

They ate breakfast in the hotel coffee shop, then took a taxi to a tall gray building on top of a hill. Their footsteps echoed down long hallways as they made their way to her doctor's office.

Inside, as they waited, Chase looked out the window to the hospital across the parking lot. "This reminds me of my internship."

Kyla pressed her knuckles together. "Did you like it?" she asked.

He shook his head. "I was in a fog. We worked long hours and when we weren't working we were on call. I probably looked the way I do today every day."

She studied the circles under his eyes, the creases around his mouth, his shaggy hair and thick eyebrows. He looked as if he hadn't slept all night. She hadn't wanted to put him through this. It was bad enough for her; but to drag someone who had no need to suffer wasn't fair.

The receptionist told them to go to an inner room and added that the doctor would be there shortly. When he finally appeared, Kyla stood, then sat down again. She opened her mouth to speak, to ask him to tell her quickly, but no sound came out.

He looked down at the file in his hands, then at her, his face empty of any expression. Time stood still.

"The gene marker is not present, Kyla. You're free of the disease."

Kyla's knees shook as she stood to face him. She felt her body shudder uncontrollably and then she started to cry. She only knew she was in Chase's arms and that her tears blended with his. She couldn't stop sobbing. She held on to him so tightly he whispered "Hey, I'm not going anywhere" in her ear.

She gulped and took a deep breath and turned to face the doctor. His eyes, too, were suspiciously red rimmed and he wiped them with a handkerchief.

"Doctor," Kyla said, holding out her hands, "you've given me my life."

Chase's face broke into a smile. He shook the doctor's hand. "You've given us our life together," he added softly.

Kyla moved to the door. "Is there a phone?"

The doctor nodded. "Outside the front door."

Kyla pulled Chase by the hand out to the hallway. She poured a fistful of coins into the telephone and put her hand over the receiver. "There are some people I want you to meet. The McDermotts of Friday Harbor. My mother's family operates on tradition and one of them is small but formal weddings in the harbor overlooking the sound. That's where my parents were married. Do you mind?"

Chase leaned against the outside of the booth and grinned at her. "Are you asking me to marry you?"

Kyla pulled him close to her, feeling her shoulder press against his chest. "No, you're asking Aunt Mildred if you can marry me. That's another tradition."

"Then why don't we go up and ask her in person?" he whispered in her ear. "Or is it traditional to do it on the phone."

Kyla smiled and shook her head. "Aunt Mildred? This is Kyla. I'm in San Francisco. I took your advice and took the test."

There was a long silence. Then Aunt Mildred spoke in a choked voice. "I can tell by your voice what the results were. When can we see you, child?"

"I'm coming up there as soon as I can. There's someone I want you to meet." There was a long, satisfied sigh from the other end of the line and Kyla could hear the dinner bell ring three times to call the family together to receive good news—another McDermott tradition.

Epilogue

The Pokhara Valley
Two Years Later

Every Nepal trek begins and ends in Kathmandu, where trekkers can visit Durbar Square and the old Royal Palace, the temples, the shops and the monasteries. But most travelers come for the majestic scenery, and the ten adults and seven children on the Adventure Family Trek were no exception. In the small village of Ghorandrum they stood and gazed transfixed at the views of Annapurna, Dhaulagiri and the "fishtail" peak of Machapuchare.

There were extra porters and Sherpas to carry tired children along well-established trails that led across valleys dotted with small villages. There was even an American doctor who carried a first-aid kit. His wife, the leader, had come out of retirement to head this special tour. She carried her own gray-eyed infant daughter in a steel-frame pack on her back. The little girl waved her arms gleefully at the mountains in the distance as if to say it wouldn't be long before she'd be up there following in her mother's footsteps.

The leader shaded her eyes and turned to her husband. He reached over her head to retie the bonnet with the wide brim on his daughter's head. Then he studied the likeness of the two women in his life—their gray eyes, unruly curls and smiles that made his heart contract.

"You're not looking at the view," Kyla said to him, her hand on his shoulder.

"Oh yes I am," Chase assured her, his gaze locked on hers. "You're still the best view Adventure Travel has to offer."

She grinned. "So that's why you came on this tour—to look at me."

"I wouldn't have missed this trip for anything. Compared to our trek to the Manang Valley, this is a piece of cake. And we have views of rhododendron forests, hill farms and friendly villagers. And no bridges. What more could you want?"

"I thought you might want to go home some day," she said while Emily Tanner Cunningham cooed and gurgled on her back.

"Wherever we hang our carpet is home. Maybe one day we'll go back to California—but not to the city. To an area where they need doctors. Is that okay with you, Emily?" he asked the baby.

"Fortunately she's very adaptable," Kyla assured him.

He smiled. "Just like her mother."

Kyla turned to watch the sun set on the snow-covered mountains, the lofty abode of the gods. And she said a silent prayer of thanks for the gift of life.

* * * * *

From *New York Times* Bestselling author Penny Jordan, a compelling novel of ruthless passion that will mesmerize readers everywhere!

Penny Jordan

Silver

Real power, true power came from Rothwell. And Charles vowed to have it, the earldom and all that went with it.

Silver vowed to destroy Charles, just as surely and uncaringly as he had destroyed her father; just as he had intended to destroy her. She needed him to want her . . . to desire her . . . until he'd do anything to have her.

But first she needed a tutor: a man who wanted no one. *He* would help her bait the trap.

Played out on a glittering international stage, Silver's story leads her from the luxurious comfort of British aristocracy into the depths of adventure, passion and danger.

AVAILABLE NOW!

SIL-1A

You'll flip . . . your pages won't! Read paperbacks *hands-free* with

Book Mate • I

The perfect "mate" for all your romance paperbacks

Traveling • Vacationing • At Work • In Bed • Studying • Cooking • Eating

Perfect size for all standard paperbacks, this wonderful invention makes reading a pure pleasure! Ingenious design holds paperback books OPEN and FLAT so even wind can't ruffle pages—leaves your hands free to do other things. Reinforced, wipe-clean vinyl-covered holder flexes to let you turn pages without undoing the strap...supports paperbacks so well, they have the strength of hardcovers!

Pages turn WITHOUT opening the strap.

Reinforced back stays flat.

Built in bookmark.

10" x 7¼", opened.
Snaps closed for easy carrying, too.

Available now. Send your name, address, and zip code, along with a check or money order for just $5.95 + .75¢ for delivery (for a total of $6.70) payable to Reader Service to:

Reader Service
Bookmate Offer
3010 Walden Avenue
P.O. Box 1396
Buffalo, N.Y. 14269-1396

Offer not available in Canada
***New York residents add appropriate sales tax.**

BM-GR

PASSPORT TO ROMANCE VACATION SWEEPSTAKES

OFFICIAL RULES

SWEEPSTAKES RULES AND REGULATIONS. NO PURCHASE NECESSARY.

HOW TO ENTER:

1. To enter, complete this official entry form and return with your invoice in the envelope provided, or print your name, address, telephone number and age on a plain piece of paper and mail to: Passport to Romance, P.O. Box #1397, Buffalo, N.Y. 14269-1397. No mechanically reproduced entries accepted.
2. All entries must be received by the Contest Closing Date, midnight, December 31, 1990 to be eligible.
3. Prizes: There will be ten (10) Grand Prizes awarded, each consisting of a choice of a trip for two people to: i) London, England (approximate retail value $5,050 U.S.); ii) England, Wales and Scotland (approximate retail value $6,400 U.S.); iii) Caribbean Cruise (approximate retail value $7,300 U.S.); iv) Hawaii (approximate retail value $ 9,550 U.S.); v) Greek Island Cruise in the Mediterranean (approximate retail value $12,250 U.S.); vi) France (approximate retail value $7,300 U.S.).
4. Any winner may choose to receive any trip or a cash alternative prize of $5,000.00 U.S. in lieu of the trip.
5. Odds of winning depend on number of entries received.
6. A random draw will be made by Nielsen Promotion Services, an independent judging organization on January 29, 1991, in Buffalo, N.Y., at 11:30 a.m. from all eligible entries received on or before the Contest Closing Date. Any Canadian entrants who are selected must correctly answer a time-limited, mathematical skill-testing question in order to win. Quebec residents may submit any litigation respecting the conduct and awarding of a prize in this contest to the Régie des loteries et courses du Quebec.
7. Full contest rules may be obtained by sending a stamped, self-addressed envelope to: "Passport to Romance Rules Request", P.O. Box 9998, Saint John, New Brunswick, E2L 4N4.
8. Payment of taxes other than air and hotel taxes is the sole responsibility of the winner.
9. Void where prohibited by law.

PASSPORT TO ROMANCE VACATION SWEEPSTAKES

OFFICIAL RULES

SWEEPSTAKES RULES AND REGULATIONS. NO PURCHASE NECESSARY.

HOW TO ENTER:

1. To enter, complete this official entry form and return with your invoice in the envelope provided, or print your name, address, telephone number and age on a plain piece of paper and mail to: Passport to Romance, P.O. Box #1397, Buffalo, N.Y. 14269-1397. No mechanically reproduced entries accepted.
2. All entries must be received by the Contest Closing Date, midnight, December 31, 1990 to be eligible.
3. Prizes: There will be ten (10) Grand Prizes awarded, each consisting of a choice of a trip for two people to: i) London, England (approximate retail value $5,050 U.S.); ii) England, Wales and Scotland (approximate retail value $6,400 U.S.); iii) Caribbean Cruise (approximate retail value $7,300 U.S.); iv) Hawaii (approximate retail value $ 9,550 U.S.); v) Greek Island Cruise in the Mediterranean (approximate retail value $12,250 U.S.); vi) France (approximate retail value $7,300 U.S.).
4. Any winner may choose to receive any trip or a cash alternative prize of $5,000.00 U.S. in lieu of the trip.
5. Odds of winning depend on number of entries received.
6. A random draw will be made by Nielsen Promotion Services, an independent judging organization on January 29, 1991, in Buffalo, N.Y., at 11:30 a.m. from all eligible entries received on or before the Contest Closing Date. Any Canadian entrants who are selected must correctly answer a time-limited, mathematical skill-testing question in order to win. Quebec residents may submit any litigation respecting the conduct and awarding of a prize in this contest to the Régie des loteries et courses du Quebec.
7. Full contest rules may be obtained by sending a stamped, self-addressed envelope to: "Passport to Romance Rules Request", P.O. Box 9998, Saint John, New Brunswick, E2L 4N4.
8. Payment of taxes other than air and hotel taxes is the sole responsibility of the winner.
9. Void where prohibited by law.

© 1990 HARLEQUIN ENTERPRISES LTD. RLS-DIR

Celiac

VACATION SWEEPSTAKES

MONTH 2 ENTRY

Official Entry Form

Yes, enter me in the drawing for one of ten Vacations-for-Two! If I'm a winner, I'll get my choice of any of the six different destinations being offered — and I won't have to decide until after I'm notified!

Return entries with invoice in envelope provided along with Daily Travel Allowance Voucher. Each book in your shipment has two entry forms — and the more you enter, the better your chance of winning!

Name ______________________________

Address ______________________________ Apt.

City ______________ State/Prov. ______________ Zip/Postal Code

Daytime phone number ______________________________
Area Code

☐ I am enclosing a Daily Travel Allowance Voucher in the amount of $__________ Write in amount revealed beneath scratch-off

© 1990 HARLEQUIN ENTERPRISES LTD.

PASSPORT
WIN
1 of 10 Vacations
SEE INSIDE
TO ROMANCE

VACATION SWEEPSTAKES

MONTH 2 ENTRY

Official Entry Form

Yes, enter me in the drawing for one of ten Vacations-for-Two! If I'm a winner, I'll get my choice of any of the six different destinations being offered — and I won't have to decide until after I'm notified!

Return entries with invoice in envelope provided along with Daily Travel Allowance Voucher. Each book in your shipment has two entry forms — and the more you enter, the better your chance of winning!

Name ______________________________

Address ______________________________ Apt.

City ______________ State/Prov. ______________ Zip/Postal Code

Daytime phone number ______________________________
Area Code

☐ I am enclosing a Daily Travel Allowance Voucher in the amount of $__________ Write in amount revealed beneath scratch-off

CPS-TWO